PENN'S CAVE

THE GARDEN OF THE GODS

PENN'S CAVE

PENNSYLVANIA'S GRANDEST CAVERN AND BEAUTIFUL LAKE KAROONDINHA

HISTORY AND LEGENDS COMPILED BY
HENRY W. SHOEMAKER

CATAMOUNT
PRESS

an imprint of Sunbury Press, Inc.
Mechanicsburg, PA USA

CATAMOUNT
PRESS

an imprint of Sunbury Press, Inc.
Mechanicsburg, PA USA

For information about special discounts for bulk purchases, please contact Sunbury Press Orders Dept. at (855) 338-8359 or orders@sunburypress.com.

To request one of our authors for speaking engagements or book signings, please contact Sunbury Press Publicity Dept. at publicity@sunburypress.com.

FIRST CATAMOUNT PRESS EDITION: March 2023

Set in Adobe Garamond | Interior design by Crystal Devine | Cover by Lawrence Knorr | Edited by Lawrence Knorr.

Publisher's Cataloging-in-Publication Data
Names: Shoemaker, Henry W., author.
Title: Penn's Cave : Pennsylvania's grandest cavern and beautiful Lake Karoondinha / History and Legends compiled by Henry W. Shoemaker.
Description: First trade paperback edition. | Mechanicsburg, PA : Catamount Press, 2023.
Summary: Henry Wharton Shoemaker's legendary guide to Penn's Cave in Centre County, Pennsylvania, includes many myths and legends sure to provide entertainment to spelunkers.
Identifiers: ISBN : 979-8-88819-071-5 (softcover) | ISBN : 979-8-88819-072-2 (ePub).
Subjects: TRAVEL / United States / Northeast / Middle Atlantic (NJ, NY, PA) | FICTION / Fairy Tales, Folk Tales, Legends & Mythology | FICTION / Cultural Heritage | FICTION / Small Town & Rural | FICTION / Short Stories.

Product of the United States of America
0 1 1 2 3 5 8 13 21 34 55

Continue the Enlightenment!

Front cover image: Penn's Cave entrance circa 1920 from an old postcard.

There is a cave
All overgrown with trailing, odorous plants,
Which curtain out the day with leaves and flowers,
And paved with veined emerald, and a fountain,
Leaps in the midst with an awakening sound;
From its curved roof, the mountain's frozen tears,
Like snow or silver or long diamond spires,
Hand downward, raining forth a doubtful light;
And there is heard the ever-moving air,
Whispering without from tree to tree, and birds,
And bees, and all around are mossy seats,
And the rough walls are cloth with long, soft grass.

—PROMETHEUS UNBOUND.

BY THE SAME AUTHOR:

Wild Life in Central Pennsylvania (1903)
Pennsylvania Mountain Stories (1907)
Philosophy of Jake Haiden (1911) (Editor)
More Pennsylvania Mountain Stories (1912)
The Indian Steps (1912)
Tales of the Bald Eagle Mountains (1912)
Susquehanna Legends (1913)
In the Seven Mountains (1914)
The Pennsylvania Lion (1914)
Wolf Days in Pennsylvania (1914)
Black Forest Souvenirs (1914)
A Week in the Blue Mountains (1914)
Pennsylvania Deer and Their Horns (1915)
A Pennsylvania Bison Hunt (1915)
Captain Logan (1915)
Juniata Memories (1916)
The Last of the War Governors (1916)
Pennsylvania Wildcats (1916)
Eldorado Found (1916)
Extinct Pennsylvania Animals, Part I (1916)
Early Potters of Clinton County (1916)

* * *

Immaterial Verses (1898)
Random Thoughts (1899)
Pennsylvania Mountain Verses (1907)
Elizabethan Days (1912)

* * *

Legend of Penn's Cave (pamphlet) (1907)
Story of the Sulphur Spring (pamphlet) (1912)
Stories of Pennsylvania Animals (pamphlet) (1913)
Stories of Great Pennsylvania Hunters (pamphlet) (1913)

CONTENTS

ILLUSTRATIONS

I

PREFACE

PENN'S CAVE needs more panegyrics and panegyrists. Beautiful natural curiosity that it is, it is hidden away among rolling hills and towering mountains, almost like "a flower to blush unseen." Having visited many of the principal caves in the United States and foreign countries and compared them with Penn's Cave, the writer of these lines has concluded that something adequate should be written concerning the great central Pennsylvania cavern. Though not having the spare time to go into the subject in detail, he has compiled the following chapters in the hope of filling the want until the proper historian can take up the subject, using the contents of this book as a foundation for more solid research and exposition. But this is sometimes difficult, as history loves to follow beaten paths. After much painstaking research and a world of care, the writer prepared the first complete history of the Pine Creek or Fort Horn Declaration of Independence. It was a subject glossed over by most Pennsylvania historians, even by the immortal Menginness. A week or so ago, in the *Romances of Pennsylvania History* series in a leading

Philadelphia newspaper, the old story was republished, just as it was given, fragmentary and imperfect, in every old history. Either the compiler of the article disregarded a newer and more complete version or did not see it, or history is too dogmatic to leave its channels. In the case of Penn's Cave, its amplified story appears on these pages for the first time; it cuts out the channel, as it were.

Consequently the writer feels an added responsibility, for here is a lack of the minuteness so characteristic of some other specimens of cave literature, notably Hovey's works. But in lieu of other treatises, these pages are presented to the public in the hope that they may answer a few of the questions about the cave and preserve the folklore clustered about it. To the writer, these pages have a deep import, as Penn's Cave determined his course to collect and preserve, if possible, the dying legends and folktales of the Pennsylvania mountains. Twenty-two years ago this month, as a little red-headed boy, he made the acquaintance of an aged Seneca Indian, Isaac Steele, who was visiting familiar scenes in the West Branch and Bald Eagle Valleys. The venerable man sat on the trunk of a felled Indian appletree at the corner of the old Quiggle orchard at McElhattan (Clinton County) and recounted the "Legend of Penn's Cave." For eleven years, it tossed about in the writer's mind until he could no longer contain it, so he wrote it down. It was first published in the *Centre Reporter* at Centre Hall (Centre County) and became the nucleus of other legends, which came out in book form in 1903 under the title *Wild Life in Central Pennsylvania*. Later editions of this book were published under the name of *Pennsylvania Mountain*

Stories, the last in 1911. And from that time on, when the writer had a little leisure, and a chance to travel, he has been collecting and "writing down" more Pennsylvania legends. Therefore, with more than the usual heartbeats, he is giving forth his latest brochure on *Penn's Grandest Cavern*. The writer wishes to extend his hearty thanks to Mr. R. P. Campbell, one of the proprietors of the cave, for the valuable assistance rendered in preparing this book and to Mr. S. W. Smith, editor of the *Centre Reporter*, for furnishing some of the most interesting illustrations.

HENRY W. SHOEMAKER
Altoona Tribune Office
Sept. 28, 1914

INTRODUCTION
to the Sixth Edition

THE demand for still another edition of this little brochure on wonderful Penn's Cave is not so much a compliment to the book as to the growing popularity and efficient management of the cavern. The inevitable destruction of Naginey Cave by quarriers, and the garnish artificial illumination of other Pennsylvania caverns, has made Penn's Cave a class by itself. This, together with the facility of visiting it by automobile, has made it the Mecca for all Pennsylvania travelers. "Meet me at the Cave" is a slogan familiar to all dwellers in "Eldorado Found," as central Pennsylvania is sometimes called. The register maintained at the cave office contains many noted names, and one must argue himself unknown not to be recorded upon its pages. The writer considers himself privileged to have figured as the humble chronicler of this great natural wonder of his beloved state. But with improved state highways, even better days are ahead. More and more people will visit Penn's Cave until it ranks as one of the best-known wonders of the American continent. Now that a waterway has been opened for boats from the cave into

Lovel Lake Karoondinha, it has become the ideal pleasure trip in Central Pennsylvania. Imperfect as the following pages are, the compiler thanks past, present, and future readers for their consideration of his efforts.

H.W.S.
Department of State
Washington, D. C.
February 24, 1930

FOREWORD
to the Seventh Edition

HENRY Wharton Shoemaker (1880–1958) was quite a character. Born into a wealthy Manhattan family, he attended Columbia College but dropped out. Rather than pursue a finance business with his brother, he gravitated to his grandparents' estate in the mountains of central Pennsylvania. Henry spent many years at this place he dubbed Restless Oaks. From there, he penned his famous stories. Penn's Cave is about 30 miles southwest (as the bald eagle flies) of Shoemaker's mountain home, and he included it in his legends. In 1914, he assembled this guidebook concerning the caves and spent much more time on invented tales of yore than the sciences of speleology and geology or spelunking techniques. Rather, Henry preferred the remembrances of lovers lost in the cave and tales allegedly told to him as a boy by an old Seneca Indian. The value of this work is not the accuracy of the tales but rather the charm of the early descriptions of the cave and the allure of its mysteries. Shoemaker was among the best storytellers and one of Pennsylvania's best writers from the early 20th century. While the veracity of the history he reveals should always be questioned, these yarns entertain today as much as they did in 1914 or throughout the years. Enjoy this popular guidebook to Penn's Cave, now in its 7th edition.

LAWRENCE KNORR
Boiling Springs, Pennsylvania
March 2023

II

DESCRIPTION

THOUGH perhaps lacking in the exquisite stalactite formations of the Crystal Cave at Virginsville, the huge "dragon" stalagmite at Dreibelbis Cave, the "Red Panther's Funeral Pyre" stalagmite in the Caves of Cobum, or the symmetry of the bush-hammered walls of the Naginey Cave, Penn's Cave excels all other Pennsylvania caverns by the vastness of its dimensions, its water trip, its diversity of formations. While other caves in the commonwealth rely on one feature of commanding interest, Penn's Cave has first-class attractions by the score. It contains so much that is of interest that it always gives fresh and absorbing pleasure even to persons who have visited it a dozen times—like the writer of this article.

First of all, let it be said that the entrance is the most imposing of any cave in the United States—maybe in the world. The flight of steps to the vast limestone arch with the depth of green water beneath it is something never to be forgotten. The boat ride, a quarter of a mile or more each way, is finer by far than the Echo River, the Styx or Lethe in Mammoth Cave in Kentucky, the Lake in Cahow Cave, or the boat ride in Smuggler's Cave in Bermuda, where Annette Kellerman posed for the great moving picture play *Neptune's Daughter*.

The mysterious abruptness with which Penn's Cave comes out into Lake Karoondinha adds greatly to its charm. The writer has crawled far into the labyrinths beyond the ending of the "watery" part, been confused by the multiplicity of passages, and been lulled by the musical echoes of countless subterranean waterfalls.

The Cave has three, possibly four or five entrances. The main entrance, already referred to, is like the doorway to the Labyrinth of the Minotaur in Auguste Gendron's famous painting, the entrance from the old orchard into the dry cave, and another which can be noticed by the ray of light which filters into one of the hidden chambers at the rear of "watery cave" are curiously picturesque. Other cork-screw or spiral apertures are observable in the ceilings at certain parts of the cavern, but as they admit no light, they cannot be definitely called "entrances."

In some places, the water attains a depth of forty feet and is a peculiar transparent greenish color. Trout and other fish find their way into the cave but do not multiply, as there is no food of importance inside; yet the earlier explorers reported that it was fairly alive with trout.

Daniel Ott of Selinsgrove, who died in 1916, aged 96 years, had stated that before the dams were built in the Susquehanna River, shad were taken in Penn's Cave. In the coldest part of winter, screech owls take refuge in the cavern. Small crayfish, rats, mice, bats, and numerous insects, including white katydids, still inhabit it in considerable numbers. Unfortunately, the bats do not hibernate in as great quantity as formerly. The noises, the acetylene lights, and the inquisitive tourists have driven these shy creatures to unknown hiding places, though their desertion is not as complete as at the charming Crystal Cave in Berks County, where the proprietor installed a system of glaring electric lighting. At dusk in summer, beginning in May, numbers of bats can be seen flitting about near the mouth of the Cave and on the green before the hotel, chasing insects. Thanks to their tireless efforts, there is an almost entire absence of mosquitoes in the vicinity of Penn's Cave. No wonder Texas has put a perpetual closed season on our little satan-winged friends. It is said that, their work done, the bats return to the cave through the small openings in the orchard, preferring it to the larger or main entrance.

According to the stories told by the first explorers, the "Dry" Cave was formerly much dryer than at present. In the old days, panthers, red bears, bob cats, foxes, and smaller mammals, made it a headquarters; the larger beasts fought for its possession. Indians sometimes camped in the Dry Cave in very cold winters. They would find it uncomfortably wet now.

The quality of the limestone composing the cave walls is very unusual. It shades from whites to delicate greys into rich pinks and reds. It is the most gorgeously colored cavern in the eastern states. Italians might almost call it "the American Capri." In some parts, the delicacy of the gray-green tones reminds one of the famous French "art nouveau" introduced at the time of the Paris Exposition in 1900. In other places, the reds are reminiscent of the richness of the best in Indian art. This is best seen in the curious, natural mural painting called *Indian Riding Pony*, which is shown to visitors on the "return trip" in the Cave. It is a "sumac" red which holds the attention just as the primitive artists evidently sought, knowing that the impressions must be given by only one color.*

The stalactites are not as numerous as in many caves, notably Luray, the Endless Caverns near Newmarket, Va., or the Wyandot Cave on the Rothrock estate in southern Indiana. Countless numbers were broken off during the dark days when there was no absolute rule in the cave and when visitors did pretty much as they pleased. The early explorers spoke enthusiastically of the stalactites, so we must blame the generation of vandals if our cave is exceeded in this respect by other American caverns. Some of the curious stalactite forms, like "The Lancaster County Tobacco Barn" and "The Lobster's Claw," are not to be excelled anywhere. But there are few transparent pendants, loveliest of all stalactites.

The stalagmite forms are finer and more numerous than the stalactites, at least in their present-day condition. They represent a wide diversity of forms, some of them, like the "Giant Pillars," being of impressive proportions, while others, like the "Prairie Dogs," are quaint and amusing in the extreme. As a "freak" formation, the "Ruffles, Scalloped" is well worth a visit. There are several places where the formations emit musical sounds upon being struck.

One great charm of Penn's Cave is that the visitor never leaves disappointed, as with many caves. The imagination,

---
* See Chapter IX.

it seems, cannot picture anything like it. Many people imagine Niagara Falls to be a grander sight than it seems at first glimpse, but on subsequent visits, it appears to grow to the proportions of the preconceived mental image. Penn's Cave comes upon the eye very differently from any prior conception; subsequent visits make it seem lovelier, weirder, and grander. Its situation in a picturesque region adds greatly to its attractiveness.

In 1898 when the writer first visited the cave, there was much original timber, white pine, white oak, and hemlock standing in the ravines adjacent to the property. Now, alas! Much of this is gone, but a quaint old-world, out-of-time atmosphere is still connected with the region.

At night to lie on the hillside by the creek that runs from the cavern, as the writer has done, and watch the Brush Mountain above so immovable and vast, frowning like a tall sentinel upon the cave property, while down in some sink a whippoorwill is improvising, or a fox barking on a distant "bench," is a rare treat to an impressionable soul which seeks the infinite.

The cave is best visited at dusk or after nightfall if the full effect of the eerie surroundings is desired. The formations appear huger, the distances greater, and the shadows more impenetrable after dark outside. Then to emerge again into the seemingly excessively warm air, into darkness, and hear a distant kildeer's mournful note or to see a bat flit mechanically over one's head are experiences in keeping with one's bewitched mental attitude.

The glory of the autumn coloring in the cave woods or on the adjoining farm is wonderful. Fall is the best time of the year to visit the great natural wonder. Many hardwoods are still standing; the hickories, in particular, are radiantly yellow in September and October. Blue jays, newly arrived from the north, cry out buoyantly.

In Maytime, the orchards and fields about the cave are a mass of white and pink sweet-scented blooms. Bird songs in the rising inflection are everywhere. The very earth smells sweet; world hopes come into our breasts. But there is a tang in the air in autumn; it comes from the drying leaves, the cracking nut burrs, and the hardening earth, which gives us a stronger grip on life. Nature is our friend in Maytime; we understand her mood, and she seems to be helping us.

In the autumn, she appears to be drawing away, becoming more distant and forgetful of us. We reverence her as more all-powerful; we feel more self-reliant. Our imaginations, for these reasons, are soothed in spring and keenly awakened in the fall. Apart from Nature's grandeur, the wonders of the cave formation hold us more "in chill October." How great a joy if one could visit the Cave on Hallowe'en!

Care should be taken to have every wonderful formation pointed out. They are well-named; not one can we afford to miss. Only after seeing them can a correct estimate be formed of Penn's Cave and its position relative to other caverns. We believe the discerning observer is bound to give it a very high place. Although the lamented Rev. Horace C. Hovey omitted to mention it in his classic work, *Celebrated American Caverns*, published in 1882, it is not too late to record Penn's Cave in the "underground hall of fame." Gradually its popularity is growing; its distinctive marvels are showing out more boldly.

Since the "mystery passage" which baffled Indian and white explorers alike from the cave into beautiful Lake Karoondinha has been opened for boats, like a genius half understood, modest, and retiring, it is coming to its own. The height of the roof in the highest part is 55 feet; the water at its greatest depth is 35 feet at the time of high water. The cave's temperature all year round is 50 degrees, and the cave property is 1,200 feet above sea level.

The cave received its name because John Penn's Creek, rightly named the Karoondinha, rises in it. Penn's Creek was named after John Penn (1729-1795), grandson of the founder of Pennsylvania, Captain James Potter having given it this appellation in January 1764. It is stated that when the view of the expansive plains of Penn's Valley first burst upon his vision from the mountain above the present town of Centre Hall, he exclaimed, "I have discovered an empire!" A legend of one of John Penn's visits to central Pennsylvania will be found in the compiler's *More Pennsylvania Mountain Stories* in the chapter entitled "Marsh Marigold."

For the benefit of the intending visitors, below is appended a list of the leading named formations, 36 in all, but hundreds of others await their "great American identifiers," which are full of strangeness, full of charm, and tonics for the imagination.

SEEN AS YOU ENTER THE CAVE	SEEN AS YOU RETURN
1 The Eagles' Wings	1 Water Falls With Lighthouse Above
2 The Lobster's Claw	2 The Ruffles, Scalloped
3 Statue of Liberty	3 North Pole Scene
4 We have No Bananas	4 Indian Riding Pony
5 Garden of Gods	5 Leopard Skins
6 The Lace Curtain	6 The Billiken
7 The Strait of Gibraltar	7 Lebanon Bologna
8 Petrified Lion	8 Boy Driving Cow Across Suspension Bridge
9 Coral Growths	9 Indian Women Carrying Papoose
10 The Chimes	10 King Tut's Stenographer Carrying Jug of Water
11 Drop Curtain	11 Wild Pigeon Wing
12 Prairie Dogs	12 Angel Wings
13 Snow Slides	13 Silver Rock
14 Pittsburg Snow Drift	14 Shadow Statue of Liberty
15 Niagara Falls (Canadian and American Sides)	15 Elephant's Head
16 Trout Colored Stalactite	
17 Turtle Shell	
18 Lancaster County Tobacco Barn	
19 Hindoo Idols	
20 Giant Pillars	

AT THE PANTHER SKINS

III

HISTORY

IT is not generally known that the namesakes, or perhaps distant relatives of America's greatest poet, Edgar Allan Poe, were the first settlers to own Penn's Cave in Centre County. These hardy frontiersmen, who fought the Indians in the mountains of Maryland and Pennsylvania, took up many tracts of land in the Pennsylvania mountains and became citizens of prominence. The original name was spelled Poh but became altered, like many other old-time names, into its present form.

The Penn's Cave farm, or tract of land as it was known in the early days, was surveyed in pursuance of two warrants granted to James Poh, or Poe, dated January 5 and November 3, 1773. The Commonwealth of Pennsylvania issued a patent for these lands to James Poe, dated April 9, 1789. James Poe only lived on the Penn's Cave farm for a short time, spending most of his days at his homestead in the valley bearing his name in the southern part of Centre County. But he built a substantial log house near the large spring where the Karoondinha emerges from the cave, the first improvement in that part of the valley.

James Poe, at his death, left the cave farm to his daughter Susanna M. Poe, and his will is duly recorded in the records of Franklin County, Pennsylvania, Centre County not yet having come into existence. The young heiress became the wife of Samuel Vantries, and the Penn's Cave farm took the name of "Vantries Place," by which name it was known for many years. Samuel Vantries lived formerly near what is now Linden Hall, and the family name is still well known in that locality. Dr. James Vantries of Bellefonte was a direct descendant of Samuel Vantries and James Poe.

There is no record that Edgar Allan Poe, during his famous visit to central Pennsylvania in 1838, ever paid a visit to his namesake at Penn's Cave. Before this trip, he was residing in Philadelphia and was on the *Gentlemen's Magazine* staff. He needed money, was heavily in debt, and thought his wealthy namesakes in the mountains would help him. He visited Poe Valley and later crossed the Seven Mountains to Milroy and Lewistown, from which latter town he returned to Philadelphia. He was greatly impressed with the large cave on the Naginey farm near Milroy and the Mammoth Spring on the Alexander farm near Reedsville.

Samuel Vantries rented the Penn's Cave farm in about 1855, as Jacob Harshbarger was living there then. Mr. Harshbarger used to say that the first person to enter the cave was Rev. James Martin, a Presbyterian preacher, who died June 20, 1795, and is buried on the Musser farm near Penn Hall. Rev. Martin was a native of Ireland, an honor graduate of Trinity College, Dublin, and pastor of the earliest Presbyterian congregation in Penn's Valley. The old gentleman, it is said, caught a cold in the cave, from which he never fully recovered.

Previous to Rev. Martin's adventure, Indians of various tribes had frequented it, as numerous souvenirs, like arrow-heads, pottery, and beads, have been taken out of it. Malachi Boyer, a young pioneer from Lancaster County, drowned in the cave in about 1749. He had run away with Nitanee, the daughter of a powerful chief, Okocho, and was captured and paid the death penalty.*

Beginning in 1845 and continuing to 1860, people frequently went down into the dry cave through the small entrance in the old orchard. No guides accompanied the visitors, however, and on an occasion, a pair of saddle horses were found tied to the orchard fence at dusk one evening, which bore the marks of having been tied there for some time. A search was made in the dry cave, and a young man and his sweetheart were found close by the water. Their lights had failed them, and they were afraid to move, and they lost all idea of which way to get out. So they decided to wait and trust the presence of the horses to bring relief.**

In about 1860, a young Quaker named Isaac Paxton, who had resided in Chester County, became a teacher at the public school in Spring Mills. He was a nature lover and fond of taking long tramps through the hills and valleys to study birds, flowers, trees, and geological formations. Accompanied by his chum, Albert Woods, a successful agriculturalist residing at Spring Mills, he walked to Penn's Cave and entered the dry cave. The young men

* See Chapter IV.
** See Chapter VI.

became convinced that they saw a light out in the direction of the watercourse entrance. Previous to this time, there was no knowledge of the water in the "dry" cave was the same stream that rises at the cave's main entrance, nor that the two parts of the cave led into one another. Paxton and Woods came out of the dry cave, went down to the saw-mill, which stood close to where the water emerges from the cavern and from which waterpower it was run, and secured enough lumber to build a raft. They carried this lumber to the main, or present, entrance of the cave, nailed it together, and with the aid of a pine torch and a long pole, traversed the watercourse in Penn's Cave for the first time. They found that the waterway led into the dry cave, unearthed the skeletons of two huge panthers, and made other interesting discoveries.* Some of the heavy sawed logs now floating at the cave's far end are supposed to be remnants of the first raft.

Presbyterian preachers must have a fondness for visiting caves, as a few days after, Rev. J. E. Long, the Presbyterian Pastor of the Valley, whose place of residence was at Hublersburg in Nittany Valley, came over and, hearing of the adventure of Messrs. Paxton and Woods, persuaded them to repeat the trip so that he might accompany them. So the three gentlemen returned to the cave, reconstructed the raft into a small boat, and traversed the gloomy waterway.

The news spread rapidly, and as the Fourth of July was approaching, a small picnic of members of "old-line" families was gotten up to spend the holiday at the cave and use the boat. The party included two aged ladies,

---

* See Chapter V.

Mrs. Margaret Foster and Miss Sarah Vanvalzah. Because of their venerable age, the compliment was paid to them of having the boat named for them, the *Sarah-Margaret*. Among those in the merry party were Miss Mary Wilson, Miss Lizzie Cook, Miss Mary Duncan, Miss Mary Woods, Miss Ada Vanvalzah, Mrs. Robert Duncan, John Foster, John Wilson, Frank Vanvalzah, Harry Vanvalzah, Dr. John Woods, Robert Duncan, and Miss Mary Buchanan.

Miss Ada Vanvalzah later became the wife of Col. John A Churchill, of St. Louis, a distinguished officer in the United States Army. Dr. John Woods practiced medicine at Boalsburg, Centre County, for many years. Miss Mary Woods, who is now living at Spring Mills, furnished the list of names of the happy party, most of whom are now enjoying their reward. Miss Ada Vanvalzah and Miss Mary Woods were the first ladies to enter the boat and go through the cave. During the day, one load would be rowed back as far as the dry cave in the rear of the cavern and left to explore the dry rooms while the boat returned for another load.

For years following this picnic, the country became so excited over the Civil War that little interest was taken in the cave until about 1870 when another picnic party visited the picturesque spot. This time the boat was hauled on a wagon from Beaver Dams, below Spring Mills, which in those days was a favorite spot for canoeists and boatmen generally. No signs were found of the old boat, the *Sarah-Margaret*.

Previous to the last picnic, in 1868, Samuel Vantries sold the farm to George Long, who lived in the old farmhouse and used the water from the "spring," which, in reality, is the overflow from the cave. Mr. Long was a man of serious nature and objected strongly to pleasure-seekers entering the cave. Furthermore, he did not want people to contaminate what he now realized was his water supply. During his regime, few people visited the cave. Upon his death in 1884, the property passed into the hands of his two sons, Jesse and Samuel. These two young men had traveled extensively and realized the financial possibilities of the cave. It was worth much more than the farm, in their estimation. In their rambles, they had visited Mammoth Cave of Kentucky, which they declared was in no way superior to their cavern. They built a larger boat and began charging admission to the cave. In 1885, they constructed the handsome building now known as the Penn's Cave Hotel. For a time, they prospered, and hundreds of people visited their unique resort annually.

In December 1895, the farm was sold to John A. Herman of Pleasant Gap, Centre County. In January 1908, the farm and cave again changed hands and became the property of its present owners. Dr. H. C. and R. P. Campbell. Previous to this, for several years, owing to financial embarrassments, the Long brothers had abandoned the hotel, and the place was deserted. The Campbell brothers, who are graduates of the Pennsylvania State College, and young men of education and foresight, improved the property extensively, making it one of the most unique resorts in central Pennsylvania. To use the words of Mr. R. P. Campbell, the active manager of the cave, "Now has come the age of the automobile, and the cave again has become a place of interest to the tourists. The number of visitors has steadily increased since we bought the place, and we expect 1914 to be the banner year."*

Penn's Cave is easy to access for residents of Altoona, especially those owning automobiles. Twenty years ago, the Naginey Cave in Milroy was visited by Altoonans every Sunday during the summer months. On several occasions, the Altoona Band waked the echoes of its dismal recesses. Since the automobile has come into use, Penn's Cave, in Centre County, can be reached as easily as the Naginey Cave in the old days. The best way to reach Penn's Cave by automobile from Altoona is to follow the main road to Tyrone, thence to Warrior's Mark, Pennsylvania Furnace, Rock Springs, State College, and Centre Hall. It is only a short distance from Centre Hall to the cave over first-class roads. Those wishing to go by train can reach Spring Mills or rising Springs Station, as it is called, on the Lewisburg and Tyrone Railroad, after changing cars at Bellefonte. Conveyances cannot always be obtained there, so it would probably be better to go by train to Centre Hall from Bellefonte. There are several excellent liveries where automobiles can be hired.

An admission fee, moderate when one considers the uniqueness of the trip by boat into the stygian depths of the cave, is charged to all visitors. This helps the upkeep of the establishment. But what appeals mostly to tourists and automobile parties is the air of courtesy and politeness that pervades the place. From Mr. Campbell down, everyone seems anxious to please, and the tired traveler will find nothing to ruffle his overstrained nerves.

---

* This prophecy proved correct, as twice as many persons visited the cave as ever before. But all records were broken in July 1916, when a veritable army of persons visited the cave; 1923 promise to be the "biggest" year of all!

THE STATUE OF LIBERTY

The scenery about the cave is magnificent; in fact, there is none finer in central Pennsylvania. The Brush Mountain comes to an abrupt end east of the cave, while to the south looms the high peaks of the Seven Mountains chain. Penn's Cave makes an ideal trip for Altoonans and gives them a chance to appreciate the matchless beauties of their native state fully. It was a place where one could find relief and rest from the cares of the modem, complex life. If the fountain of youth is in Pennsylvania, surely it must have flowed out of the unsounded depths of Penn's Cave,* for all who have been there have come away strengthened and spiritually purified by its rare beauty and a precious flood of memories.

* See Chapter VII.

IV

THE LEGEND OF PENN'S CAVE

(Related by Isaac Steele, an Aged
Seneca Indian, in 1892)

I N THE DAYS when the West Branch Valley was a
trackless wilderness of defiant pines and submissive
hemlocks, twenty-five years before the first pioneer had
attempted lodgment beyond Sunbury, a young Pennsylvania Frenchman from Lancaster County, named Malachi
Boyer, alone and unaided, pierced the jungle to a point
where Bellefonte is now located. The history of his travels
has never been written, partly because he had no companion to observe them and partly because he could not write.
His very identity would now be forgotten were it not for
the traditions of the Indians with whose lives he became
strangely entangled.

Malachi Boyer was a short, stockily built fellow with
unusually prominent black eyes and black hair that hung
in ribbon-like strands over his broad, low forehead. Fearless
yet conciliatory, he escaped a thousand times from Indian
cunning and treachery, and as the months went by and
he penetrated further into the forests, he numbered many
natives among his cherished friends.

Why he explored these boundless wilds, he could not explain, for it was not in the interest of science, as he scarcely knew of such a thing as geography, and it was not for trading, as he lived by the way. But on he forced his path, ever aloof from his race, on so the story concludes. But to his dying day, he always placed the battle of the panthers first of all his hunting adventures. And his faith in the unknown horseman as his deliverer and unknown horseman as his deliverer and good genius became the absorbing, all-pervading influence of his life.

Why he explored these boundless wilds, he could not explain, for it was not in the interest of science, as he scarcely knew of such a thing as geography, and it was not for trading, as he lived by the way. But on he forced his path, on the alert for the strange scenes that encompassed him day by day.

One beautiful month of April—no one can tell the exact year—found Malachi Boyer camped on the shores of Spring Creek. Near the Mammoth Spring was an Indian camp, whose occupants maintained a quasiintercourse with the pale-faced stranger. Sometimes old Chief Okocho would bring gifts of corn to Malachi, who in turn presented the chieftain with a hunting knife of the truest steel. And in this way, Malachi spent more and more of his time in the Indian camps, only keeping his distance at night and during religious ceremonies.

Old Okocho's chief pride was centered in his seven stalwart sons, Humkin, Hokolin, Toochin, Ostin, Chawkeebin, Ahakin, Kolopakin, and his Diana-like daughter, Nitanee. The seven brothers resolved themselves into a guard of honor for their sister, who had many suitors, among whom was the young chief Efaw from the adjoining subtribe of the Acawkotahs. But Nitanee gently, though firmly, repulsed her numerous suitors until her father would give her in marriage to one worthy of her regal blood.

Thus ran the course of Indian life when Malachi Boyer made his bed of hemlock boughs by the gurgling waters of Spring Creek. And it was the first sight of her washing a deerskin in the stream that led him to prolong his stay and ingratiate himself with her father's tribe.

Few were the words that passed between Malachi and Nitanee, many glances, and the handsome pair often met in the mossy ravines near the campgrounds. But this was all clandestine love, for friendly as Indian and white might be in social intercourse, never could marriage be tolerated until—there is always a turning point in romance—the black-haired wanderer and the beautiful Nitanee resolved to spend their lives together, and one moonless night started for the more habitable east.

All night long, they treaded their silent way, climbing the mountain ridges, gliding through the velvet-soiled hemlock glades, and wading, hand in hand, the splashing, resolute torrents. When morning came, they breakfasted on dried meat and huckleberries and bathed their faces in a mineral spring. Until—there is always a turning point in romance—seven tall, stealthy forms, like animated mountain pines, stepped from the gloom and surrounded the eloping couple. Malachi drew a hunting knife, identical to the one he had given to Chief Okocho, and, seizing Nitanee around the waist, stabbed right and left at his would-be captors. The first stroke pierced Humkin's heart, and uncomplainingly, he sank down, dying. The six remaining brothers, although receiving stab wounds, caught Malachi in their combined grasp and disarmed him; then one brother held sobbing Nitanee while the others dragged fighting Malachi across the mountain.

That was the last the lovers saw of one another. Below the mountain lay a broad valley, from the center of which rose a circular hillock, and it was to this mound the savage brothers led their victim. As they approached, a yawning cavern met their eyes, filled with greenish limestone water. There is a ledge at the mouth of the cave, about six feet higher than the water, above which the arched roof rises thirty feet, and it was from here they shoved Malachi Boyer into the tide below. He sank or a moment, but when he rose to the surface, he commenced to swim. He approached the ledge, but the brothers beat him back, so he turned and made for some dry land in the rear of the cavern. Two of the brothers ran from the entrance over the ridge to watch, where there was another small opening, but though Malachi tried his best in the impenetrable darkness, he could not find this or any other avenue of escape. He swam back to the cave's mouth, but the merciless Indians were still on guard. He climbed up again and again but was repulsed and once more retired to the dry cave. He renewed his efforts to escape every day for a week, but the brothers were never absent. Hunger became unbearable, and his strength gave way, but he vowed he would not let the redskins see him die, so forcing himself into one of the furthermost labyrinths, Malachi Boyer breathed his last.

Two days afterward, the brothers entered the cave and discovered the body. They touched not the coins in his pockets but weighted him with stones and dropped him into the deepest part of the greenish limestone water. And after these years, those who have heard this legend declare that on the still summer nights, an unaccountable echo rings through the cave, which sounds like "Nitanee, Nitanee."

V

CAVE PANTHERS

EVERYONE who has hunted in the "Seven Brothers," as the Seven Mountains are called in central Pennsylvania, has heard of Daniel Karstetter, the famous Nimrod.* Though the greater part of a hundred years have passed since he was in his heyday as a slayer of big game, his fame is undiminished. Anecdotes of his prowess are related in every hunting camp. By one and all, he has been acclaimed the greatest hunter that the Seven Brothers ever produced. The great Nimrod, who lived to a very advanced age, was born in 1818, on Pine Creek, near its confluence with Karoondinha, or Penn's Cree, at the Blue Rock, half a mile east of the present town of Coburn. In addition to his hunting prowess, he was interested in psychic experiences and was as prone to discuss his adventures with supernatural agencies as his conflicts with the wild denizens of the forest. There was a particular ghost story that he loved dearly to relate.

Accompanied by his younger brother Jacob, he had been attending a dance one night across the mountains, in the environs of the town of Milroy, for like all the

* The Seven Mountains comprise the Path Valley, Short, Bald, Thicic Head, Sand, Shade and Tussey Mountains.

backwoods boys of his time, he was adept in the art of
terpsichore. The long journey was made on horseback; the
lads mounted on stout Conestoga chargers. The homeward ride commenced after midnight, the two brothers
riding along the dark trail in single file. In the wide flat
on the top of the "Big Mountain," Daniel fell into a doze.
When he awoke, his mount having stumbled on a stone,
Jacob was nowhere to be seen. Thinking that his brother
had put his horse to a trot and gone on ahead, Daniel dis-
missed the matter of his absence from his mind. As he was
riding down the deep slope of the mountain, he noticed a
horseman waiting for him on the path. When they came
abreast, the other rider fell in beside him, skillfully guiding
his horse so that it did not encounter the dense foliage
which lined the narrow way. Daniel supposed the party to
be his brother, although the unknown kept his lynx-skin
collar turned up, and his felt cap was pulled down level
with his eyes. It was pitchy dark, so, to make sure, Daniel
called out, "Is that you, Jacob?"

His companion did not reply, so the young man
repeated his query in still louder tones, but all he heard was
the crunching of the horses' hoofs on the pebbly road.

Daniel Karstetter, master-slayer of panthers, red bears,
and wild cats, was no coward, though, on this occasion, he
felt uneasy. Yet he disliked picking a quarrel with the silent
man at his side, who clearly was not his brother, and feared
putting his horse to a gallop on the steep, uneven roadway.
The trip home never before seemed of such interminable
length. Daniel made no attempt to converse with his unso-
ciable comrade for the greater part of the distance.

Finally, he heaved a sigh of relief when he saw the light gleaming in the horse stable at the home farm. When he reached the barnyard gate, he dismounted to let down the bars while the stranger apparently vanished in the gloom. Daniel led his mount to the horse stable, where he found his brother Jacob sitting by the old tin lantern, fast asleep. He awakened him and asked him when he had gotten home. Jacob stated that his horse had been feeling good, so he let him canter all the way. He had been sleeping but judged that he had been home at least half an hour. He had met no horseman on the road. Daniel was convinced that his companion had been a ghost, or, as they are called in the "Seven Brothers." a *gshpook*. But he made no further comment that night.

A year afterward, returning from a dance in Stone Valley, he was again joined by the silent horseman, who followed him to his barnyard gate. He gave up going to dances on that account. At least once a year, or as long as he could go out at night, he met the ghostly rider. Sometimes, when tramping along on foot after a hunt or, in later years, coming back from the market in his Jenny Lind, he would find the silent horseman at his side. After the first experience, he never attempted to speak to the nightrider, but he became convinced that it meant no harm.

As his prowess as a hunter became recognized, he had many jealous rivals among the less successful Nimrods. In those old days, threats of all kinds were freely made. He heard on several occasions that certain hunters were setting out to "fix" him. But a man who could wrestle with panthers and bears knew no such thing as fear.

One night, while tramping along in Green's Valley, he was startled by some one in the path ahead of him shouting out in Pennsylvania Dutch, "Hands up!" He was on the point of dropping his rifle when he heard the rattle of hoof-beats back of him. The silent horseman, in an instant, was by his side, the dark horse pawing the earth with his giant hoofs. There was a cracking of brush in the path ahead and no more threats of *hend uff*. The ghostly rider followed Daniel to his barnyard gate but was gone before he could utter a word of thanks. As a result of this adventure, he became imbued with the idea that he possessed a charmed life. It gave him added courage in his many encounters with panthers, fierce red bears, and lynxes.

Apart from his love of hunting the more dangerous animals, Daniel enjoyed the sport of deer-shooting. He maintained several licks, one in a patch of low ground near the entrance to the "dry" part of Penn's Cave. At this spot, he construed a blind, or platform, between two ancient tupelo trees, about twenty feet from the ground, and many were the huge white-faced stags that fell to his unerring bullets during the rutting season.

One cold night, according to an anecdote frequently related by one of his descendants, while perched in his eyrie overlooking the natural clearing which constituted the lick and in sight of a path frequently by the fiercer beasts, which led to the opening of the "dry" cave, he saw, about midnight, a huge pantheress, followed by a large male of the same specie, come out into the open. The pantheress strolled from the path and came and laid herself down at the roots of the tupelo trees while the panther remained in the path and seemed to be listening to some noise as yet inaudible to the hunter. Daniel soon heard a distant roaring; it seemed to come from the very summit of Brush Mountain, and immediately the pantheress answered it. Then the panther, on the path, his jealousies aroused, commenced roaring with a voice so loud that the frightened hunter almost let go of his trusty rifle and held tighter to the railing of his blind, lest he might tumble to the earth. As the voice of the animal that he had heard in the distance gradually approached, the pantheress welcomed him with renewed roaring, and the panther, restless, went and came from the path to his flirtatious flame as though he wished her to keep silence, and from the pantheress to the path, as though to say, 'Let him come if he dares; he will find his match.'

In about an hour, a gigantic panther stepped out of the forest and stood in the full moonlight on the other side of the cleared place. The pantheress, eyeing him with admiration, raised herself to go to him, but the panther divining her intent, rushed before her and marched right at his adversary. With measured step and slowly, they approached within a dozen spaces of each other. Their smooth, round heads were high in the air, their bulging yellow eyes gleaming, their long, tufted tails slowly sweeping down the brittle asters that grew around them. They crouched to the earth—a moment's pause—and then they bounded with a hellish scream high in the air and rolled on the ground, locked in their last embrace.

The battle was long and fearful to the amazed and spellbound witness of this midnight duel. Even if he had so wished, he could not have taken steady enough aim to fire. But he preferred to watch the combat while the moonlight lasted. The bones of the two combatants cracked under their powerful jaws, their talons strewed the frosty ground with entrails and painted it red with blood, and their outcries, now guttural, now sharp and loud, told their rage and agony.

At the beginning of the contest, the pantheress crouched herself on her belly, with her eyes fixed upon the gladiators, and all the while, the battle raged, manifested, by the slow, catlike motion of her tail, the pleasure she felt at the spectacle.

When the scene closed, and all was quiet and silent and death-like on the lick, and the moon had commenced waning, she cautiously approached the battleground and, sniffing the lifeless bodies of her two lovers, walked leisurely to a nearby oak, where she stood on her hind feet, sharpening her fore claws on the bark. She glared up ferociously at the hunter in the blind as if she meant to vent her anger by climbing after him.

In the moonlight, her golden eyes appeared so terrifying that Daniel dropped his rifle, and it fell to the earth with a sickening thud. As he reached after it, the flimsy railing gave way, and he fell literally into the arms of the pantheress. Just then, the rumble of horses' hoofs, like thunder on some distant mountain, was heard. Just as the panther was about to rend the helpless Nimrod to bits, the unknown rider came into view. Scowling at the intruder mounted on his huge black horse, the brute abandoned her prey and ambled off toward the dry cave. Daniel seized his firearm and sent a bullet after her retreating form, but it went wild of its mark.

Meanwhile, before he had time to express his gratitude to the stranger, he had vanished. Daniel was dumbfounded. As soon as he recovered from the blood-curdling episodes, he built a small fire near the mammoth carcasses, warming his much-benumbed hands. Then he examined the dead panthers but found their hides too badly torn to warrant skinning. Disgusted at not getting his deer and being even cheated out of the panther pelts, he dragged the ghastly remains of the erstwhile kings of the forest by their tails to the edge of the entrance to the dry cave. There he cut off the long ears to collect the bounty and shoved the carcasses into the aperture. They fell with sickening thuds into the chamber beneath, to the evident horror of the pantheress, which uttered a couple of piercing screams as the horrid remains of the recent battle royal landed in her vicinity. Then Daniel shouldered his rifle and started out in search of small game for his breakfast.

That night he went to another of his picks on Elk Creek, where he killed four superb stags. But to his dying day, he always placed the battle of the panthers first of all his hunting adventures. And his faith in the unknown horseman as his deliverer and good genius became the absorbing, all-pervading influence of his life.

VI

THE LITTLE POSTMISTRESS

IT was long past dark when Mifflin Sargeant of the Snow Shoe Land Company came within sight of the welcoming lights of Stover's. For fourteen miles, through the foothills of the Narrows, he had not seen a sign of human habitation except one deserted hunter's cabin. There was an air of cheerfulness and life about the building where he had arrived. Several doors opened simultaneously at the signal of his approach, given by a faithful watchdog, throwing the rich glow of the fat lamps and tallow candles across the road.

The structure, which was very long and two stories high, housed under its accommodating roof a tavern, a boarding house, a farmstead, a lumber camp, a general store, and a post office. It was the last outpost of civilization in the east end of Brush Valley; beyond were mountains and wilderness almost to Youngmanstown. Tom Tunis had not yet erected the substantial structure on the verge of the forest, later known as "The Forest House." A dark-complexioned lad, who later proved to be Reuben Stover, the landlord's son, took the horse by the bridle, assisting the young stranger to dismount. He also helped unstrap his saddlebags, carrying them into the house.

As he passed across the porch, Sargeant noticed that the walls were closely hung with stags' horns, which showed the prevalence of those noble animals in the neighborhood. Old Daddy and Mammy Stover ran the quaint caravansery and quickly made the visitor feel at home. It was after the regular suppertime, but a fresh repast was prepared in the huge stone chimney cheerfully. The young man explained to his hosts that he had ridden that day from New Berlin; he had come from Philadelphia to Harrisburg by train, to Liverpool by packet boat, at which last-named place his horse had been sent on to meet him. He added that he was on his way into Centre County, where he had recently purchased an interest in the Snow Shoe development.

After supper, he strolled along the porch to the far end, to the post office, thinking he would send a letter home. A mail had been brought in from Redersburg during the afternoon; consequently, the post office, and not the tavern stand, attracted the crowd this night. The narrow room was poorly lit by fat lamps, which cast great, fitful shadows, making grotesques out of the oddly-costumed, bearded wolf hunters present, who were the principal inhabitants of the surrounding ridges. A few women, hooded and shawled, were noticeable in the throng. In a far corner, leaning against the water bench, was young Reuben, the hostler, tuning up his wheezy fiddle. As many persons as possible hung over the rude counter, across which the mail was being delivered, and where many letters were written in reply. Above this counter were suspended three fat lamps, attached to grooved poles, which, by cleverly-devised pulleys, could be lifted to any height desired. The young Philadelphian edged his way through the good-humored concourse to ask permission to use the ink; he had bought his favorite quill pen and the paper with him. This brought him face to face, across the counter, with the postmistress. He had not been able to see her before, as her little trim figure had been wholly obscured by the ponderous forms that lined the counter.

Instantly he was charmed by her appearance—it was unusual—by her look of neatness and alertness. Their eyes met—it was almost with a smile of mutual recognition. When he asked her if he could borrow the ink kept in a large, earthen pot of famous Sugar Valley make, she smiled at him again, and he absorbed the charm of her personality anew. Though she was below the middle height, her figure was so lithe and erect that it fully compensated for the lack of inches. She wore a blue homespun dress with a neatly checked apron over it, the material for which constituted a luxury and must have come all the way from Youngman-stown or Sunbury. Her profuse masses of soft, wavy, light-brown hair, on which the hanging lamps above brought out a glint of gold, was worn low on her head. Her deep-set eyes were a transparent blue, her features well developed, and when she turned her face in profile, the high arch of the nose showed at once mental stability and energy. Her complexion was fair; there seemed to be always that kindly smile playing about the eyes and lips.

When she pushed the heavy inkwell toward him, he noticed that her hands were very white, the fingers

THE CHIMES

tapering; they were the hands of innate refinement. Almost imperceptibly, the young man found himself in conversation with the little postmistress. Doubtless, she was interested in meeting an attractive stranger from such a distant city as Philadelphia. While they talked, the letter was gradually written, sealed, weighed, and paid for; it was before the days of postage stamps, and the postmistress politely waited on her customers. He had told her his name—Mifflin Sargeant—and she had given him hers—Caroline Hager—and that she was eighteen years of age. He had told her about his prospective trip into the wilds of Centre County, of the fierce beasts which he had heard still abounded there. The girl informed him that he would not have to go farther west to meet wild animals; that wolf hides by the dozens were brought to Stover's every winter where they were traded in; that old Stover, a justice of the peace, attested to the bounty warrants—in fact, the wolves howled from the hill across the road on cold nights when the dogs were particularly restless. Her father was a wolf hunter and would never allow her to go home alone; consequently, when he could not accompany her, she remained in the dwelling which housed the post office. Panthers, too, were occasionally met with in the locality (in the original surveys, the region was referred to as "catland"), also huge red bears and the somewhat smaller black ones. If he was going west, she continued in her pretty way; he must not fail to visit the great limestone cave near where the Brush Mountain ended. She had a sister married and living not far from it, from whom she had heard wonderful tales, though she had never been there herself. It was a cave so vast it had not as yet been fully explored; one could travel for miles in it in a boat; John Penn's Creek had its source in it; Indians had formerly lived in the dry parts, and wild beasts. Then she lowered her voice to say it was now haunted by the Indians' spirits.

And so they talked until a very late hour, the crowd in the post office melting away, until Jared Hager, the girl's father, in his wolfskin coat, appeared to escort her home to the cabin beyond the waterfall near the trail to Hope Valley. She was to have a holiday until the next afternoon. The wolf hunter was a courageous-looking man, much darker than his daughter, with a heavy beard and bushy eyebrows. He spoke pleasantly with the young stranger, and then they all said good night.

"Don't forget to visit the great cavern," Caroline called to the youth.

"I surely will," he answered, "and stop here on my way east to tell you all about it."

"That's good; we want to see you again," said the girl as she disappeared into the gloomy shadows the shaggy white pines cast across the road.

Young Stover was playing "Green Grows the Rushes" on his fiddle in the taproom, and Sargeant sat there listening to him, dreaming and musing all the while, his consciousness singularly alert until the closing hour came. That night, in the old cold stained four-poster, in his tiny, cold room, he slept not at all. Yet he "feared to dream." Though his thoughts carried him all over the world, the little postmistress was uppermost in every fancy. Among other things, he wished that he had asked her to ride with him to the cave. They could have visited the subterranean marvels together. He got out of bed and managed to light the fat lamp. By its sputtering gleams, he wrote her a letter, which ended abruptly as the small supply of ink he carried with him was exhausted. But as he repented of the intense sentences penned to a person who knew him so slightly, he arose before morning and tore it to bits.

There was a white frost on the buildings and ground when he came downstairs. The autumn air was cold; the atmosphere was a hazy, melancholy grey. There seemed to be a cessation of all the living forces of nature as if waiting for the summons of winter. From the chimney of the old inn came he pungent odor of burning pine wood.

With a strange sadness, he saddled his horse and resumed his ride toward the west. He constantly thought of Caroline—so much so that after he had traveled ten miles, he wanted to turn back; he felt miserable without her. If only she were riding beside him, the two bound for Penn's Valley Cave, he could be supremely happy. Without her, he did not care to visit the cavern or anything else, so at Madisonburg, he crossed the northern Mountains, leaving the southerly valleys behind.

He rode up Nittany Valley to Bellefonte, where he met he agent of the Snow Shoe Company. He visited the vast tract opening to lumbering, mining, and colonization with this gentleman. But his thoughts were elsewhere; they were across the mountains with the little postmistress of Stover's.

Satisfied that his investment would prove remunerative, he left the Development Company's cozy lodge house and, with his heart growing lighter with each mile, started for the east. It was wonderful how differently—how vastly more beautiful the country seemed on this return journey. He fully appreciated the wistful loveliness of the fast-fading autumn foliage, the crispness of the air, the beauty of each stray tuft of asters, the last survivors of the wild flowers along the trail. The world was full of joy; everything was in harmony.

Again it was after nightfall when he reined his horse in front of Stover's long, rambling house. This time two doors opened simultaneously, sending forth golden lights and shadows. One was from the taproom, where the hostler emerged; the other from the post office, bringing little Caroline. There was no mail that night; consequently, the office was practically deserted; she had time to come out and greet her much-admired friend. And let it be said that her heart was aflame with the image of Mifflin Sargeant ever since she had seen him. She was canny enough to appreciate such a man; besides, he was a good-looking youth, though perhaps of a less robust type than those most admired in the Red Hills.

After cordial greetings, the young man had his supper, after which he repaired to the post office. By that time, the last straggler was gone; he had a blissful evening with his fair Caroline. She anticipated his coming, being somewhat of a psychic, and had arranged to spend the night with the Stovers. They were in no hurry to retire; when they went out on the porch preparatory to locking up, the hunter's moon was sinking behind the western knobs, which rose like the pyramids of Egypt again the skyline.

Sargeant lingered around the old house for three days;
when he departed, it was with extreme reluctance. Seeing
Caroline again in the future appeared like something too
good to be true, so downhearted was he at the parting.
But he had arranged to come back the following autumn,
bringing an extra horse with him, and the two would ride
to the wonderful cavern in Penn's Valley and explore to the
ends its stygian depths. Meanwhile, they would make the
most of their separation through steady correspondence.
Despite glances, the pressure of hands, chance caresses,
and evident happiness in one another's society, not a
word of love had passed between the pair. That was why
the pain of parting was so intense. If Caroline could have
remembered one loving phrase, she would have felt that
she had something tangible to hang her hopes. If the young
Philadelphian had unburdened his heart by telling her that
he loved her and her alone and heard her words of affir-
mation, the world out into which he went riding would
have seemed less a blank. But underneath his love, burning
like a hot branding iron, was his consciousness of class,
his fear of the consequences if he took to the great city a
bride from another sphere. As an only son, he could not
picture himself deserting his widowed mother and sisters
and living at Snow Shoe; there, he was sure that Caroline
would be happy. Neither could he see permanent peace of
mind if he married her and brought her into his exclusive
circle in the Quaker City. As he was an honorable young
man, and his love was real, making her truly and always
happy was the solitary consideration.

These thoughts marred the parting; they blistered
and ravaged his spirit on the whole dreary way back to

Liverpool. There his servant was waiting at the old Susquehanna House to ride the horse to Philadelphia. The young
man boarded the packet, riding on to Harrisburg, where
he took the steam train home. In one way, he was hap-
pier than ever before in his life, for he had found love; in
another, he was the most dejected of men, for his beloved
might never be his own.

He seemed gayer and stronger to his family; evidently,
the trip into the wilderness had done him good. He had
begun his letter-writing to Caroline promptly. It was his
great solace in his heart's perplexity. She wrote a very good
letter, tender and sympathetic; the handwriting was clear,
almost masculine, denoting the bravery of her spirit.

During the winter, he was called upon through his
sisters to mingle much with the society of the city. He met
many beautiful and attractive young women, but the die of
love had been cast for him. He was Caroline's irretrievably.

Absence made his love firmer, yet the solution of it all
the more enigmatical. The time passed on apace. Another
autumn set in, but on account of important business
matters, it was not until December that Sargeant departed
for the wilds of central Pennsylvania. But he could spend
Christmas with his love.

This time he sent two horses ahead to Liverpool. When
he reached the queer old river town, he dropped into an
old saddlery shop, where the canal-boat drivers had their
harness mended and purchased a neat side saddle all stud-
ded with brass-headed nails. This he tied on behind his
servant's saddle.

The two horsemen started up the Mahantango, crossing
the Shade Mountain to Swinefordstown, thence over the

edge of Jack's Mountain to Hartley Hall and the Narrows, a slightly shorter route to Stover's. On his previous trip, he had ridden along the river to Selin's Grove, across Chestnut Ridge to New Berlin, over Shamokin Ridge to Youngmanstown, and from there to the Narrows; he was in no hurry; no dearly loved girl was waiting for him in those days.

Caroline, looking prettier than ever—she was a trifle plumper and redder cheeked—was at the post office steps to greet him. Despite his avoidance of words of love, she was certain of his innermost feelings and opined that the ultimate result would be well somehow. Sergeant had arranged to arrive on a Saturday evening so they could begin their ride to the cave that night after the post office closed and be there bright and early Sunday morning. For this reason, he had traveled by very easy stages from Hartley Hall so the horses might be fresh for their added journey.

Sargeant's devoted factotum was taken somewhat aback when he saw how attentive the young man was to the girl and marveled at the mountain maid's rare beauty. Upon instructions from his employer, he set about changing the saddles, placing the brand new lady's saddle on the horse he had been riding. It was not long until the tiny post office was closed for the night, and Caroline emerged, wearing a many-caped red riding coat, the hood of which she threw over her head to keep the wavy, chestnut hair in place. She climbed into the saddle gracefully—she seemed a natural horsewoman—and soon, the loving pair were cantering up the road towards Wolfe's Store, Rebersburg, and the cave.

It was not quite daybreak when they passed the home of old Jacob Harshbarger, the tenant of the "cave farm," a

THE GHOST ROOM

Greeley rooster was crowing lustily in the barnyard, and the unmilked cattle of the ancient black breed shook their heads lazily; no one was up. The young couple planned to visit the cave, have breakfast, spend the day with Caroline's sister, who lived not far away at Centre Hall, and ride leisurely back to Stover's in the late afternoon. It had been a cold all-night ride, but they had been so happy that it seemed brief and free from all disagreeable physical sensations.

In those days, there was no boat in the cave and no guides; consequently, all intending visitors had to bring their own torches. This Caroline had seen to, and in her leisure moments for weeks before her lover's coming, had been arranging a supply of rich-pine lights that would see them safely through the gloomy labyrinths. They fed their horses and then tied them to the fence of the orchard which surrounded the entrance to the "dry" cave and had been recently set out. Several big original white pines grew along the road and would give the horses shelter in case it turned out to be a windy day.

The young couple strolled through the orchard and down the steep path to the mouth of the "watery" cave, where they gazed for some minute at the expanse of greenish water, the high span of the arched roof, the general impressiveness one in love. How gloriously happy they were! But they did get a trifle hungry, but that was appeased at first by the remnants of the breakfast provisions, which they luckily still had in a little bundle.

When sufficient time had elapsed for the night to set in, they fell asleep in each other's arms. Caroline's last conscious moment was to feel her lover's kisses.

When they awoke, many hours afterward, they were hungrier than ever and thirsty. Sargeant fumbled about, locating a small pool of water where the two quenched their thirst. But still, they were happy, come what may. They would be rescued, that was certain, unless the horses had broken loose and run away, but there was small chance of that. They had been securely tied. It was strange that no one had seen the steeds in so long a time, with the farmhouse less than a quarter of a mile away—but it was at the foot of the hill.

Hunger grew apace with every hour. After a while, drinking water would not sate it. It throbbed and ached; it became a dull pain that only love could triumph over.

Again enough hours elapsed to bring sleep, but it was harder to find repose, though Sargeant's kisses were marvelous recompense. Caroline never whimpered from lack of food. To be with her lover was all she asked. She had prayed for over a year to be with him again. She would be glad to die at his side, even of starvation. The young man was content: hunger was less painful to him than the past fourteen months' separation.

Again came what they supposed to be morning. They knew there must be some way out near at hand, as the air was so pure. They shouted, but the dull echoes were their only reward. Strangely enough, they had never felt another cold gust like the one which had blown out their torches. Could the shade of one of the old-time Indians who had fought for possession of the cave be the perpetrator of the trick, suggested lovely little Caroline? If so, she thought to herself; he had helped her, not harmed her, for could there be in the world a sensation half so sweet as sinking to rest in her handsome lover's arms?

Meanwhile, the world outside the cavern had been going its way. Shortly after the young equestrians passed the Harshbarger dwelling, all the family had come out. After attending to their farm duties, they drove off to the Seven Mountains, where the family's sons maintained a hunting camp on the Karoondinha on the other side of High Valley. The boys had killed an elk; consequently, the guests remained longer than expected to partake in a grand Christmas feast.

They tarried at the camp all that day and all of the next; it was not until early on the morning of the third day that they started back to the Penn's Cave farm. They had arranged with a neighbor's boy, Mosey Shell, who lived further along the creek below the farmhouse, to do the feeding in their absence; it was winter; there was no need to hurry home.

When they got home, they found Mosey watering two dejected, dirty-looking horses with saddles on their backs.

"Where did they come from" shouted the big freight-wagon load in unison.

"I found them tied to the fence up at the orchard. By the way, they act, I'd think they hadn't been watered or fed for several days," replied the boy.

"You dummy!" said old Harshbarger in Dutch. "Somebody's in that cave, got lost, and can't get out."

He jumped out of the heavy wagon and ran to a corner of the corncrib, where he kept a stock of torches. Then he hurried up the steep hill towards the entrance to the dry cave. The big man was panting when he reached the opening, where he paused to kindle a torch. Then he lowered himself into the pit, shouting at the top of his voice, "Hello! Hello! Hello!"

It was not until he had gotten into the first chamber that the captives in the inner room could hear him. Sargeant had been sitting with his back propped against the cavern wall while Caroline, very pale and white-lipped, was laying across his knees, gazing up into the darkness, imagining that she could see his face. When they heard the cheery shout of their deliverer, they did not instantly attempt to scramble to their feet. Instead, the young lover bent over; his lips touched Caroline's, who instinctively had raised her face to meet his. As his lips touched hers, he whispered, "I love you, my darling, with all my heart.

We will be married when we get out of here." Caroline had time to say, "You are my only love," before their lips came together.

They were in that position when the flare of farmer Harshbarger's torch lit up their hiding place. Pretty soon, they were on their feet and, with their rescuer, figuring out just how long they had been in their prison—their prison of love. They had gone into the cave on the morning of December 24th; it was now the morning of the 27th, almost noon. Christmas had come and gone. Caroline still had enough strength to climb up the tortuous passage, though her lover did help her some, as all lovers should.

The farmer's wife had some coffee and buckwheat cakes ready when they arrived at the manse, which the erstwhile captives of Penn's Cave sat down to enjoy. As they ate, another of Harshbarger's sons rode up on horseback. He had been to the post office at Earlysburg. He handed Sargeant a tiny, badly typed newspaper published in Millheim. Across the front page, in letters larger than usual, were the words, "Mexico Declares War with the United States."

Sargeant scanned the headline intently, then laid the paper on the table. "Our Country has been drawn into a war with Mexico," he said, trembling with emotion. "I had hoped it might be avoided. I am First Lieutenant of the Lafayette Greys; I fear I'll have to go."

Caroline lost the color that had returned to her pretty cheeks since emerging from the underground dungeon. She reached over, grasping her lover's now clammy hand. Then noticing no one was listening, she said faintly: "It is terrible to have you leave me now, but won't you marry me before you go? I do love you."

"Certainly I will," replied Sargeant, with enthusiasm. "I will have more to fight for, with you at home bearing my name."

Love had broken the bonds of caste.

VII

GOVERNOR CURTIN'S VISIT

CAPTIAN JOHN Q. DYCE,* one of the pioneer Democratic leaders of Clinton County, who died in 1904, was fond of telling about Governor Andrew G. Curtin's visit to Penn's Cave and the great statesman's opinion of the cavern. It appeared that during the Philadelphia Centennial in 1876, among hosts of other celebrated foreigners who visited the exposition were three Russians of note, Field Marshal von Fersen, Count Hickoff, and Baron de Toplitz-Herberstain. They were accompanied by their secretaries and retinues of servants. The heat of the city was intolerable—it was in August—and, tiring of the marvels of the exposition, they sought to visit the interior of the state in search of cooler weather.

One of the party recalled the fact that a few years previously, Andrew G. Curtin, who lived somewhere in central Pennsylvania, had been in Russia as United States Minister. The Russians admired the gallant "War Governor," who had made a most efficient envoy so that nothing would satisfy them but seek out and pay him their respects. And thus, it came to pass that one night, when the Bald

---

* He was an officer of the "Battalions" before the Civil War.

Eagle Valley train pulled into Bellefonte, it deposited on
the platform to the wonder of the collected natives, three
Russian grandees, nine lesser individuals, and a pile of lug-
gage mountain-high.

It so happened that ex-Govemor Curtin was at home
alone, the rest of his family being at Saratoga. The ticket
agent informed the great statesman that some foreigners,
who spoke very little English, were waiting for him at the
station. Hurrying to the depot as fast as he could travel,
he recognized his intending guests, who embraced him in
turn. They accepted the proffered invitation to spend the
night at the War Governor's mansion, and soon the entire
party was riding up the hill in a hotel bus, commandeered
for the purpose.

Once in the commodious mansion, the Russians felt
perfectly at home. First, they salaamed many times before
Brookman's magnificent oil portrait of Czar Nicholas II,
which the "Little Father" had graciously presented to Curtin before he departed from St. Petersburg, which hung
in the War Governor's library. The visitors were much
impressed by the dry, cool, pine-laden air, which reminded
them, they said, so much of Russia. These remarks made the
tactful Curtin decide that the best form of entertainment
would be a drive into the surrounding country. With his
truly matchless memory, he recollected that Count Hickoff
was a man of some scientific attainments, had been one of
the party to unearth the skeleton of a mammoth in Siberia,
the tusks of which had been sent to the Stuttgart museum,
measured on the outside curve twelve feet ten and one-half
inches, and had the greatest circumference of thirty-one

AN INTERIOR VIEW OF THE DRY CAVE

and one-half inches. Doubtless, the noblemen would enjoy an excursion to the Penn's Cave, situated within a delightful driving distance of Bellefonte.

Captain Dyce happened to be in town that night to discuss the Tilden Campaign with the War Governor. Governor Curtin, who was naturally too busy with his Russian guests to talk politics, smilingly told the Clinton County leader that he could do him a great favor if the next morning at eight o'clock, he would have five or six two-horse surreys in front of the Curtin home. Dyce took the hint and spent the entire night among the local liverymen and horse jockeys getting together the equipment.

The next morning, which dawned delightfully clear, at seven-thirty, found six dignified-looking two-horse surreys, each driven by a grinning driver, lined up on the hilly street before the War Governor's domicile. As the party emerged from the house, the governor addressed them, saying: "Gentlemen, we go this morning to the greatest natural wonder in Pennsylvania."

The Russian dignitaries, who were great horse lovers, spent fully fifteen minutes inspecting the livery nags, a goodly lot of trotting-bred type, which they declared were on the same general lines of their own Orloffs. As he got in his carriage, Field Marshal von Fersen, who owned a vast stock farm on the Volga, shook his head sadly, saying: "What a pity you Americans don't keep your horses entire."

Frequently on the drive, the distinguished tourists uttered exclamations of delight at the grand scenery and prosperous-looking farms, but they were kept laughing most of the way at the jokes, and humorous anecdotes told them by Governor Curtin and Captain Dyce, both of whom had inherited inimitable wit from their Celtic ancestors.

Arriving at the Penn's Cave Farm, the party was cordially received by proprietor George Long and his wife. Mr. Long was one of Governor Curtin's political admirers; consequently, he whispered to his spouse to prepare the best dinner she knew how.

While it was getting ready, the party, led by the proprietor, was taken through the cavern in a huge flatboat. The emotional Russians kept shouting with approbation while Count Hickoff, a fine singer, woke the echoes with the Russian National Anthem. The visit to the dry cave was particularly edifying to all concerned. Count Hickoff collected a pocketful of bones and shells while the hospitable proprietor Long broke off several of the choicest stalactites for him.

"You say that this is Pennsylvania's greatest natural wonder?" said Baron de Toplitz-Herberstain, as the party emerged into the warm sunlight: "but I say there is nothing finer in Russia, or perhaps in the world."

At these words, Governor Curtin smiled, as he was an early believer in the theory of "seeing America first" and dearly loved his native central Pennsylvania. The Pennsylvania country dinner served by Mrs. Long and her handmaidens was fully up to the traditions of such a repast. It is stated that nine kinds of pie were on the table at one time. And that each Russian sampled them all.

Before going to the cave, Governor Curtin had explained the "caste" system of Russia to the Longs;

consequently, only the three grandees, their secretaries, the governor, and Captain Dyce sat down at the "first table." The Russians conversed with the Longs in High German, being replied to in Pennsylvania Dutch. The rest of the party, including the drivers and the Long family, were at the second table, and there was aplenty for all.

After the dinner, which was equal to any Russian wedding feast, all averred, the party was driven back to Bellefonte.

After spending another night under Governor Curtin's hospitable roof, the happy Russians departed for Altoona and Pittsburgh, loaded with letters of introduction from their host to the car builders and steel magnates whose works they wished to inspect. But in all their travels, interesting as they doubtless were, they hardly enjoyed themselves more than their trip to "Pennsylvania's greatest natural wonder," Penn's Cave.

VIII

THE FOUNTAIN OF YOUTH

OLD CHIEF WISAMEK, of the Kittochtinny Indians, had lost his spouse. He was close to sixty years of age, which was old for a native, especially one who had led the hard life of a warrior, exposed to all kinds of weather, fasts, and forced marches. Though he felt terribly lonely and depressed in his state of widowerhood, the thought of discarding the fidelity of the eagle, which, if bereaved, never takes a second mate, and was the noble bird he worshiped, was repugnant to him until he happened to see the fair and buxom maid Annapalpeteu. He was rheumatic, walking with difficulty; he tired easily and was fretful, all sure signs of increasing age, but what upset him most was the sight of his reflection in his favorite pool, a haggard, wizened, wrinkled face with a nose like the beak of an eagle, and eyes as colorless as clay.

When he opened his mouth, the reflected image seemed mostly toothless; the lips were blue and thin. He had noticed that he did not need to shave his skull anymore to give prominence to his warrior's top knot; the proud tuft itself was growing sparse and weak; to keep it erect, he was now compelled to braid it with hair from the buffalo's tail.

Brave warrior that he was, he hated to pay his court to the lovely Annapaleteu when on all sides, he saw stalwart six-foot youths, masses of sinews and muscle, clear-eyed, firm-lipped, always ambitious and high-spirited. But one afternoon, he saw his copper-colored love sitting by the side of the Bohundy Creek, beating maize in a wooden trough. Her entire costume consisted of a tight petticoat of blue cloth, hardly reaching the knees and without any ruffles. Her cheeks and forehead were neatly daubed with red. She seemed very well content with her coadjutor, a bright young fellow, who was quite as naked as the ingenuous beauty except for two wildcat hides appropriately distributed.

That Annapalpeteu has a cavalier was now certain, and immediately it rekindled what flames remained in his jaded body; he must have her at any cost. Down by the Conadogwinet, across the Broad Mountains, lived Mbison, a wise man. Old Wisamek would get there and consult him, perhaps obtain some potion to permanently restore at least a few of the fires of his lost youth. Though his willpower had been appreciably slackening of late years, he acted with alacrity on visiting the soothsayer.

Before sundown, he was on his way to the south, accompanied by several faithful henchmen. He carried a long ironwood staff and moved on with unwonted agility; it was very dark and the path difficult to follow when he finally consented to bivouac for the night.

The next morning found him so stiff that he could hardly clamber to his feet. His henchmen assisted him, though they begged him to rest for a day. But his will

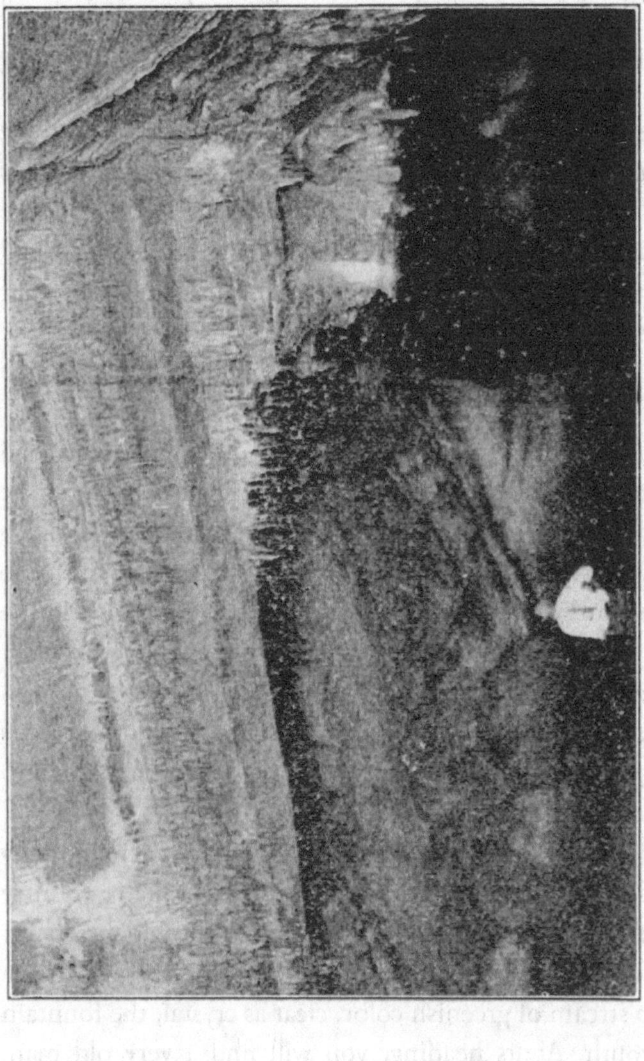

THE JEWELED CHAMBER

forced him on; he wanted to be virile and win the beautiful Annapalpeteu.

The journey, which consumed a week, cost the aged Strephon a world of effort. But as he had been indefatigable in his youth, he was determined to reach the wise man's headquarters, walking like a warrior and not carried there on a litter like an old woman. Bravely he forged ahead, his aching joints paining miserably until, at length, he came in sight of his Promised Land. The soothsayer, who had been apprised of his coming by a dream, was in front of his substantial lodge-house to greet him. Seldom had he received a more distinguished client than Wisamek, so he welcomed him with marked courtesy and deference.

After the first formalities, the old chief, who had restrained himself with difficulty, asked how he could be restored to a youthful condition so that he could rightfully marry a beautiful maiden of eighteen summers. The wise man, who had encountered similar supplicants in the past, informed him that the task was comparatively easy. It would involve, however, another journey across mountains. Wisamek shouted for joy when he heard these words and impatiently demanded where he would have to go to be restored to youth.

"Across many high mountain ranges, across many broad valleys, across many swift streams, through a country covered with dark forests and filled with wild beasts, to the northwest of here, is a wonderful cavern. In it rises a deep stream of greenish color, clear as crystal, the fountain of youth. At its heading, you will find a very old man, Gamunk, who knows the formula. Give him this talisman, and he will allow you to bathe in the marvelous waters and be young again."

With the final words, he handed Wisamek a red bear's tooth, on which was cleverly carved the form of an athletic youth. The old chief's hands trembled so much that he almost dropped the precious fetich. But he soon recovered his self-control and thanked the wise man. Then he ordered his henchmen to give the soothsayer gifts, which they did, loading him with beads, pottery, wampum, and rare furs. Despite the invitation to remain until he was completely rested, Wisamek determined to depart at once for the fountain of youth. He was so stimulated by his high hope that he climbed the steep ridges, crossed the turbulent streams, and put up with the other inconveniences of the long march much better than might have been the case.

During the entire journey, he sang Indian love songs, strains which had not passed his lips in thirty years. His followers, gossiping among themselves, declared that he looked better already. Perhaps he would not have to bathe in the fountain after all. He might resume his youth because he willed it so. Indians were strong believers in the power of mind over matter.

When he reached the vicinity of the cave, he was fortunate enough to meet the aged Indian who was its guardian. Though his hair was snow white, he said he was so old that he had lost count of the years. Gamunk's carriage was erect, his complexion smooth, his eyes clear and kind. He walked along with a swinging stride, very different from Wisamek's mental picture of him. The would-be bridegroom, who handed him the talisman, was quick to impart his mission to his new-founded friend. "It is true," he replied; "after a day and a night's immersion in the cave's water, you will emerge with all the appearance of youth. There is absolutely no doubt of it. Thousands have been here before."

With these reassuring words, Wisamek again leaped for joy, gyrating like a young brave at a cantico. The party, accompanied by the old guardian, quickly arrived at the cave's main opening, where beneath them lay stretched the calm, mirror-like expanse of greenish water.

"Can I begin the bath now?" asked the chief impatiently. "I am anxious to throw off the odious appearance of age."

"Immediately," replied the old watchman, who took him by the hand, leading him to the ledge where it was highest above the water. "Jump off here," he said quietly.

Wisamek, who had been a great swimmer in his youth and was absolutely fearless of the water, replied that he would do so.

"But remember, you must remain in the water without food until this hour tomorrow," said the guardian.

As he leaped into the water depths, the chief shouted he would remain twice as long if he could be young again. Wisamek was true to his instructions; there was too much at stake; he dared not falter.

The next morning his henchmen were at the caves' mouth to greet his reappearance. They were startled to see a tall and handsome man climbing up the ledge with alacrity, as young looking as themselves. There was a smile on the full, red lips, a twinkle in the clear eye of the remade warrior as he stood among them, physically a prince among men.

The homeward journey was made with rapidity. Wisamek traveled so fast that he played out his henchmen, who were half his age. Annapalpeteu, seated in front of her parent's cabin, weaving a garment, noticed a youth of great physical beauty approaching at the head of Chief Wisamek's clansmen. She wondered who he could be as he wore Wisamek's headdress of feathers of the sea eagle.

When he drew near, he saluted her and, not giving her time to answer, joyfully shouted, "Don't you recognize me? I am your good friend Wisamek, come back to win your love, after a refreshing journey through the distant forests."

Annapalpeteu, who was a sensible enough girl to have admired the great warrior for his prowess, even though she had never thought of him seriously as a lover, was now instantly smitten by his engaging appearance. The henchmen withdrew, leaving the couple together. They made marked progress with their romance; words of love were mentioned before they parted.

It was not long before the betrothal was announced, followed shortly by the wedding festival.

At the nuptials, the bridegroom's appearance was the marvel of all present. It was hinted that he had been somewhere and renewed his youth, but as the henchmen were sworn to secrecy, how it had been done was not revealed. The young bride seemed radiantly happy. She had every reason to be; the other Indian maids whispered from lip to lip, was she nor marrying the greatest warrior and hunter of his generation, the most handsome man in a hundred tribes?

Secretly envied by all of her age, possessing her stalwart prize, the fair bride started on her honeymoon, showered with acorns and good wishes. So far as is known, the wedding trip passed off blissfully. There were smiles on the bright faces of both bride and groom when they returned to their spacious new lodge-house, which the tribe had erected for them in their absence by the banks of the rippling Bohundy.

But the course of life did not run smoothly for the pair. Though outwardly, Wisamek was the most handsome and youthful looking of men; he was still an old man at heart. Annapalpeteu was a pleasure-loving as she was beautiful. She wanted to dance and sing and mingle with youthful company. She wanted her good time in life; her joy of living was at its height, her sense of enjoyment at its zenith.

On the other hand, Wisamek hated all forms of gaieties or youthful amusements. He wanted to sit about the lodge-house in the sun, telling of his warlike triumphs of other days; he wanted to sleep much; he hated noise and excitement.

Annapalpeteu, the dutiful wife she was, tried to please him, but over time, both husband and wife realized that romance was dying, that they were drifting apart. Wisamek was even more aware of it than his wife. It worried him greatly; his dreams were unhappy. He pictured the end of it all, with his wife, Annapalpeteu, in love with someone else of her own age, someone whose heart was young. He had spells of moodiness and irritability, as well as several serious quarrels with his wife, whom he accused of caring less for him than formerly. The relations became

VIEW ALONG THE KAROONDINHA

so strained that life in the commodious lodge-house was unbearable.

At length, it occurred to Wisamek that he might again visit the fountain of youth, this time to revive his soul. Perhaps he had not remained on the water long enough to touch the spirit within. He informed his spouse that he was going on a long journey, on the invitation of the chief of a distant tribe, and that she must accompany him. He was insanely jealous of her now; he could not bear her out of his sight. He imagined she had a young lover hiding back of every tree, though she was honor personified.

The trip was made pleasantly enough, as the husband was in better spirits than usual. He thought he saw the surcease of his troubles ahead of him!

When he reached the Beaver Dam meadows, near the site of the present town of Spring Mills, beautiful level flats which in those days were a favorite camping ground for the red men, he requested the beautiful Annapalpeteu to remain there for a few days, that he was going into a hostile country, he would not jeopardize her safety. He was going on an important mission that would make her love him more than ever when he returned.

In reality, no unfriendly Indians were about, but to give a look of truth to his story, he left her in charge of a strong bodyguard. Wisamek's late conduct had been so peculiar that his wife was not sorry to see her lord and master go way. Handsome though he was, a spiritual barrier had arisen between them, which grew more insurmountable with each succeeding day. Yet, when he was out of her sight, she felt apprehensive about him on this occasion.

She had a strange presentment that she would never see him again.

Wisamek was filled with hopes; his spirits had never been higher as he strode along, followed by his henchmen. When he reached the top of the path which led to the mouth of the cave, he met old Gamunk, the guardian. The aged wise man expressed surprise at seeing him again.

"I have come for a *very* peculiar reason," he said. "The bath I took last year outwardly made me young, but only outwardly. Within, I am as withered and joyless as a centenarian. I want to bathe once more, to try to revive the old light in my soul."

Gamunk shook his head. "You may succeed; I hope you will. I never heard of anyone daring to take a second bath in these waters. The tradition of the hereditary guardians, of whom I am the hundredth in direct succession, has it that it would be fatal to take a second immersion, especially to remain in the water for twenty-four hours." Then he asked Wisamek for the talisman, which was the right to bathe.

Wisamek drew himself up proudly and, with a gesture of his hand, indicating disdain, said he had no talisman and would bathe anyhow. He advanced to the brink and plunged in.

Until the same hour the next day, he floated and paddled about the greenish depths, filled with expectancy. For some reason, it seemed longer this time than on the previous visit.

At last, by the light which filtered down through the treetops at the cave's mouth, he knew that the hour had

come for him to emerge—emerge as Chief Wisamek—
young in heart as in body. Proudly he grasped the rocky
ledge and swung himself out on dry land; he arose to his
feet. His head seemed very light and giddy. He fancied he
saw visions of his old conquest, old loves. There was the
sound of music in the air. Was it martial music played to
welcome the conqueror or the wind surging through the
feathery tops of the maple and linden trees at the mouth of
the cave? He started to climb the steep path. He seemed to
be treading on air. Was it the buoyant steps of youth come
again? He seemed to float rather than walk. The sunlight
blinded his eyes. Suddenly he had a flash of normal consciousness. He dropped to the ground with a thud like an
old pine falling. Then all was blackness, silence. Jaybirds
complaining in the trees alone broke the stillness.

His bodyguards, who were waiting for him at old
Gamunk's lodge house, close to where the hotel now
stands, became impatient at his non-appearance as the
hour passed. Accompanied by the venerable watchman,
they started down the path. To their horror, they saw the
dead body of a hideous, wrinkled old man, all skin and
bones, lying stretched out across it, a few steps from the
entrance to the cave.

When they approached closer, they noticed several
familiar tattoo marks which identified the body as that of
their late master, Wisamek. Frightened lest they would be
accused of his murder and shocked by his altered appearance, the bodyguards turned and took to their heels. They
disappeared into the trackless forests to the north and were
never seen again.

Old Gamunk, out of pity for the vain glorious chieftain, buried the remains by the path near where he fell.

As for poor Annapalpeteu, the beautiful, she waited patiently for many days by the Beaver Dams, but her waiting was in vain. At length, concluding that he had been slain in battle in some valorous encounter, she started for her old home on the Bohundy.

It is related that in due course of time, she married a warrior of her own age, living happily ever afterward. In him, she found the loving response, the congeniality of pleasure which had been denied the dried, feeble soul of Wisamek, who bathed once too often in the fountain of youth.

IX

RIDING HIS PONY

WHEN Rev. James Martin visited Penn's Cave in the spring of 1795, it was related that he found a small group of Indians encamped there that evening, around the campfire; one of them related a legend of one of the curiosities of the watery cave, the flamboyant "Indian Riding Pony" mural-piece which decorates one of the walls. Spirited as a Remington, it bursts upon the view, creates a lasting impression, then vanishes as the power skiff, the *Nitanee*, draws nearer.

According to the old Indians, there lived not far from where the Karoondinha emerged from the cavern, a tribe who made this delightful lowland their permanent abode. While most of their cabins were huddled near together on the stream's upper reaches, there were straggling huts clear to the Beaver Dams. The finding of arrow points, beads, and pottery along the creek amply attests to this.

Among the clan was a maiden named Quetajaku, not good to look upon but in no way ugly or deformed. She was light-hearted and sociable in her youth, with a gentle disposition. Yet, for some reason, she was not favored by

SCENES FROM PENN'S CAVE PROPERTY

the young bucks. All her contemporaries found lovers and husbands, but poor Quetajaku was left severely alone. She knew that she was not beautiful. Though she was of good size, she was equally certain she was not a physical monster. She could not understand why she could find no the vastness of the night.

On one occasion, an Indian artist named Niganit, an undersized old wanderer, appeared at the lonely woman's home. For a living, he decorated pottery, shells, and bones and sometimes even painted war pictures on rocks. Quetajaku was so kind to him that he built himself a lean-to on the slope of the hill, intending to spend the winter.

On the long winter evenings, the lone woman confided to the wanderer the story of her unhappy life, of her inward consolation. She said that she had longed to meet an artist who could carry out a certain part of her dream, which had a right to come true.

When she died, she had arranged to be buried in a fissure of rocks that ran horizontally into one of the walls of the "watery" cave. On the opposite wall, she would like painted a portrait of a handsome young warrior in the most brilliant colors, with arms out-stretched coming towards her.

Niganit said that he understood what she meant exactly but suggested that the youth be mounted on a pony, a beast that was coming into use as a mount for warriors, of which he had lately seen a number in his travels on the Virginia Coast. The idea pleased Quetajaku, who authorized the stranger to begin work at once. She saved up a little property of various kinds: she promised to bestow all of this on

Niganit, except what would be necessary to bury her if the picture proved satisfactory.

The artist rigged up a dog raft with a scaffold on it, and he poled into the place where the fissure was located, the woman accompanying him the first time, so there would be no mistake.

All winter long, by torchlight, he labored away. He used only one color, an intensive brick-red made from mixing sumac, a kind of seed, a small root, and the bark of a tree, as being more permanent than that made from ochres and other ores or stained earth. Marvelous and vital was the result of this early impressionist; the painting had all the action of life. The superb youth in war dress, with arms outstretched, on the agile war pony, was rushing towards the foreground, almost leaping from the rocky panel into life, across the waters of the cave to the arms of his beloved. It would make old Quetajaku happy to see it, she who had never known love or beauty. The youth in the mural typified what Niganit would have been himself were he the chosen and what the old squaw would have possessed had nature favored her. It was the idea for two disappointed souls.

Breathlessly the old artist ferried Quetajaku to the scene of his endeavors. When they reached the proper spot, he held his quavering torch aloft. Quetajaku, to see more clearly, held her two hands above her eyes. She gave a little cry of exclamation, then turned and looked at Niganit intently. Then she dropped her eyes, beginning to cry to herself. The artist looked at her fine face, down which the tears were streaming, and asked her the cause of her grief— was the picture such a terrible disappointment?

The woman drew herself together, replying that it was grander than she had anticipated, but the face was Niganit's and, strangely enough, was the face she had dreamed of all her life.

"But I am not the heroic youth you pictured," said the artist sadly. "I am sixty years old, stoop-shouldered, and one leg is shorter than the other."

"But that is how you would look on your war pony; it is your face, shoulders, and arms. You are the picture that I always hoped would come true."

Niganit looked at the Indian woman. She was not hideous; there was even a dignity to her large, plain features, her great gaunt form. "I have never received praise such as yours. I always vowed I would love the woman who really understood me and my art. I am yours. Let us think no more of funeral decorations but go to the east, to the land of the war ponies, and ride to endless joy together."

Quetajaku, overcome by the majesty of his words, leaned against his massive shoulder. In that way, he poled his dog raft against the current to the cave's entrance. There was a glory in the reflection from the setting sun over against the east; the night would not set in for an hour or two. And towards the darkening east that night, two happy travelers could be seen wending their way.

GRAVE OF REV. JAMES MARTIN
(near Penn Hall, Centre County) One of the first white men to enter Penn's Cave

X

NITANEE

(A Tradition of a Juniata Maiden)

O NE of the last Indians to wander through the Juniata Valley, either to revive old memories or merely to hunt and trap, his controlling motive is not certain, was old Jake Faddy. As he was supposed to belong to the Seneca tribe and spent most of his time on the Coudersport Pike on the borderline between Clinton and Potter Counties, it is to be surmised that he never lived permanently on the Juniata but had hunted there or participated in the bloody wars in the days of his youth. He continued his visits until he reached a very advanced age. Of a younger generation than Shaney John, he was nevertheless well acquainted with that unique old Indian and always spent a couple of weeks with him at his cabin on Saddler's Run.

Old Jake, partly to earn his board and partly to show his superior knowledge, was a gifted storyteller. He liked to obtain the chance to spend the night at farmhouses where there were aged people, and his smattering of history would be fully utilized to put the older folks in good humor.

While the hard-working younger generations fancied that history was a waste of time, the old people loved it and fought against the cruel way all local traditions and legends were being snuffed out. If it had not been for a few people carrying it over the past generation, it would now be lost in the whirlpool of a commercial, materialistic age. And to those few, unknown to fame and of obscure life and residence, is due the credit of saving for us the wealth of folklore that the noble mountains, the dark forests, the wars, and the Indians, instilled in the minds of the first settlers. And there is no old man or woman living in the wilderness without a story ready to be imparted and worthy of preservation. But the question remains, how can these old people all be reached before they pass away? It would take an army of collectors to work simultaneously, as the Grim Reaper is hard at work removing these human landmarks with their unrecorded stories.

Near the heading of Beaver Dam Run, at the foot of Jack's Mountain, stands a very solid-looking stone farmhouse, a relic of pioneer days. Its earliest inhabitants had run counter to the Indians of the neighborhood for the possession of the beavers whose dams and "cabins" were its most noticeable feature clear to the mouth of the stream, and later for the otters who defied the trappers a quarter of a century longer. Beaver trapping had made the stream a favorite rendezvous for the natives, and their campgrounds at the springs near the headwaters were pointed out until a comparatively recent date.

But one by one, the aborigines dropped away until Jake Faddy alone upheld the traditions of the people. There were no beavers to quarrel over in his day, consequently his visits were on a more friendly basis. The old North of Ireland family who occupied the stone farmhouse was closely linked with the history of the Juniata Valley, and they felt the thrill of the vivid past whenever the old Indian appeared at the kitchen door. As he was always ready to work and, what was better, a very useful man at gardening and flowers, he was always given his meals and lodging for as long as he cared to remain. But that was not very long, as his restless nature was ever goading him on, and he had "many other friends to see," putting it in his own language. He seemed proud to have it known that he was popular with a good class of people, and his ruling passion may have been to cultivate these associations. He brought some of his sons with him on several occasions, but they did not seem anxious to live up to their father's standards. And after the old man had passed away, none of this younger generation ever came to the Juniata Valley.

The past seemed like the present to Jake Faddy; he was so familiar with it. To him, it was as if it happened yesterday, the vast formations and changes and epochs. And the Indian people, especially the eastern Indians, seemed to have played the most important part in those titanic days. It seemed so recent and so real to the old Indian that his stories were always interesting. The children also were fond of hearing him talk; he had a way of never becoming tiresome. Every young person who heard him remembered what he said. There would have been no break in the "apostolic succession" of Pennsylvania legendary lore if all had been seated at Jake Paddy's knee.

Of all his stories, by odds, his favorite one dealt with the Indian maiden, Nitanee, for whom the fruitful Nittany Valley and the towering Nittany Mountain are named.

This Indian girl was born on the banks of the lovely Juniata, not far from the present town of Newton Hamilton, the daughter of a powerful chief. It was in the early days of the world when the physical aspect of Nature could be changed overnight by a fiat from the Gitchie-Manitto or Great Spirit. It was, therefore, in the age of great and wonderful things before a rigid world produced beings whose lives followed grooves as tight and permanent as the gullies and ridges.

During the early life of Nitanee, a great war was waged for the possession of the Juniata Valley. The aggressors were Indians from the south who longed for the scope and fertility of this earthly Paradise. Though Nitanee's father and his brave cohorts defended their beloved land to the last extremity, they were driven northward into the Seven Mountains and beyond. Though they found themselves in beautiful valleys filled with bubbling springs and teeming with game, they missed the Blue Juniata and were never wholly content. The father of Nitanee, Chunehoe, felt so humiliated that he only went about after night in his new home. He took up his residence on a broad plain, not far from where State College now stands, and should be the Indian patron of that growing institution instead of Chief Bald Eagle, who never lived near there and whose good deeds are far outweighed by his crimes.

Chunehoe was an Indian of exact conscience. He did his best in the cruel war, but the southern Indians must have had more sagacious leaders or a better *esprit de corps*. At any rate, they conquered. Chunehoe was not an old man at the time of his defeat, but it is related that his raven black locks turned white overnight. He was broken in spirit after his downfall and only lived a few years in his new home. His widow, daughter Nitanee, and many other children were left to mourn him. As Nitanee was the oldest, she assumed a vicereine over the tribe until her young brother, Wowinape, should be old enough to rule the councils and go on the warpath.

The defeat on the Juniata, the exile to the northern valleys, and the premature death of Chunehoe were to be avenged. Active days were ahead of the tribesmen. Meanwhile, if the southern Indians crossed the mountains to covet still further their lands and liberties, who should lead them to battle but Nitanee? But the Indian vicereine was of a peace-loving disposition. She hoped the time would never come when she would have to preside over scenes of carnage and slaughter. She wanted to see her late father's tribe become the most cultured and prosperous in the Indian world and, in that way, be avenged on their warlike foes: "Peace hath its victories."

But she was not to be destined to lead a peaceful nation through years of upward growth. In the Juniata Valley, the southern Indians had become over-populated; they sought broader territories. They had driven the present occupants of the northern valleys out of the Juniata country; they wanted to drive them again further north.

Nitanee did not want war, but the time came when she could not prevent it. The southern Indians sought to provoke a conflict by making settlements in the Bare Meadows and in some fertile patches on Tussey Knob and Bald Top, all of which were countenanced in silence. But when they

WHERE REV. MARTIN WROTE HIS SERMONS
(Musser Farm near Penn Hall)

murdered some peaceable farmers and took possession of
plantations at the foot of the mountains in the valley of
the Karoondinha, the mildness of Nitanee's cohorts ended.
Meanwhile, her mother and brother had died, and Nitanee
had been elected queen.

Every man and boy volunteered to fight; a huge army
was recruited overnight. They swept down to the settlements of the southern Indians, butchering every one of
them. They pressed onward to the Bare Meadows and
the slopes of Bald Top and Tussey Knob. There they gave
up the population to fire and sword. Crossing the Seven
Mountains, they formed a powerful cordon all along the
southerly slope of the Long Mountain. Building block
houses and stone fortifications—some of the stonework
can be seen to this day—they could not be easily dislodged.

The southern Indians, noticing the flames of the burning plantations, and hearing from the one or two survivors of the completeness of the rout, were slow to start
an offensive movement. But as Nitanee's forces showed
no signs of advancing beyond the foot of Long Mountain,
they mistook this hesitancy for cowardice and sent an
attacking army. It was completely defeated in the gorge of
Laurel Run, above Milroy, and the right of the northern
Indians to the Karoondinha and the adjacent valleys was
signed, sealed, and delivered in blood. The southern Indians were, in turn, driven out by other tribes; in fact, every
half century or so, a different people ruled over the Juniata
Valley. But in all those years, none of the Juniata rulers
sought to question the rights of the northern Indians until
1635 when the Lenni-Lenape invaded the country of the

Susquehannocks and were decisively beaten on the plains near Rock Springs, in Spruce Creek Valley, at the Battle of the Indian Steps.

As Nitanee wanted no territorial accessions, she left the garrisons at her southerly forts intact and retired her main army to its home valleys, where it was disbanded as quickly as it came together. All were glad to be back to peaceful avocations; none of them craved glory in war. And there were no honors given out, no great generals created. All served as private soldiers under the direct supervision of their queen. The theory of this Joan of Arc was that elimi-nating titles and important posts would create no military class and no ulterior motive assisted except patriotism. The soldiers serving anonymously and for their country's needs alone would be ready to end their military duties as soon as their patriotic task was done.

Nitanee regarded soldiering as a stem necessity, not an excuse for pleasure, pillage, or personal advancement. Under her, there was no nobility; all were on a common level of dignified citizenship. Every Indian in her realm had a task, not one he was born to follow, but the one which appealed to him most and, therefore, the task at which he was most successful. Women also had their work, apart from domestic life, in this ideal democracy of ancient days. Suffrage was universal to both sexes over twenty years of age, but as there were no official positions and no public trusts, a political class could not exist, and the queen, as long as she was cunning and able, had the unanimous support of her people. She was given a great ovation as she modestly walked along the fighting line after the winning battle of

Laurel Run. It made her feel not that she was great but that
the democracy of her father and her ancestors was a living
force. In those days of pure democracy, the rulers walked:
the litters and palanquins were a later development.

After the conflict, the gentle Nitanee, at the head of
the soon-to-be disbanded army, marched across the Seven
Brothers and westerly toward her permanent encampment,
where State College now stands. As her only trophy, she
carried a bundle of spears, which her brave henchmen had
wrenched from the hands of the southern Indians as they
charged the forts along Long Mountain. These were not to
deck her own lodge house nor for vain display but were to
be placed on her father's grave, the lamented Chunehoe,
who had been avenged. In her heart, she had hoped for
victory, almost as much for his sake as for the comfort of
her people. She knew how he had grieved himself to death
when he was outgeneraled in the previous war.

In those dimly remote days, there was no range of
mountains where the Nittany chain now raises their noble
summits to the sky. All was a plain, a prairie, north clear to
the Bald Eagles, which only recently had come into existence. The tradition was that far older than all the other
hills were the Seven Mountains. And geological speculation
seems to bear this out. At all seasons of the year, cruel and
chilling winds blew out of the north, hindering the work
of agriculture on the broad plains ruled over by Nitanee.
Only the strong and the brave could cope with these killing
blasts, so intense and so different from the calming zephyrs
of the Juniata. The seasons for this cause were several weeks
shorter than across the Seven Mountains; that is, there was

a later spring and an earlier fall. But though the work was harder, the soil being equally rich and broader area, the crops averaged fully as large as those further south. So, taken altogether, the people of Nitanee could not be said to be unhappy.

As the victorious queen was marching along at the head of her troops, she was frequently almost mobbed by women and children, who rushed out from the settlements and made her all manner of gifts. As it was in the early spring, there were no floral garlands but instead wreaths and festoons of laurel, ground pine, and ground spruce. There were gifts of precious stones and metals, rare furs, beautiful specimens of Indian pottery, basketry, and the like. These were graciously acknowledged by Nitanee, who turned them over to her bodyguards to be carried to her permanent abode on the "Barrens." But it was not a "barrens" in those days, but a rich agricultural region carefully irrigated from the north and yielding the most bountiful crops of Indian com. It was only when abandoned by the frugal Indians and grown up with forests that burned over repeatedly through the carelessness of the white settlers that it acquired that disagreeable name. In those days, it was known as the "Hills of Plenty."

As Nitanee neared the scenes of her happy days, she was stopped in the middle of the path by an aged Indian couple. Leaning on staffs to present a dignified appearance, it was easily seen that age had bent them nearly double. Their weazened, weatherbeaten old faces were pitiful to behold. Toothless and barely able to speak above a whisper, they addressed the gracious queen.

"We are very old," they began, "the winters of more than a century have passed over our heads. Our sons and grandsons were killed fighting bravely under your immortal sire, Chunehoe. We have had to struggle on by ourselves as best we could ever since. We are about to set out a crop of corn, which we need badly. For the past three years, the north wind has destroyed our crop every time it appeared; the seeds we plan to put in the earth this year are the last we've got. Really, we should have kept them for food, but we hoped that the future would treat us more generously. We want a windbreak built along the northern side of our corn patch; we are too feeble to go to the forests and cut and carry the poles. Will not our most kindly queen have someone assist us?"

Nitanee smiled at the aged couple; then, she looked at her army of able-bodied warriors.

Turning to them, she said, "Soldiers, will a hundred of you go to the nearest royal forest, which is in the center of this plain, and cut enough cedar poles with brush on them to build a wind-break for these good people?"

Instantly a roar arose, a perfect babel of voices; every soldier was trying to volunteer for this philanthropic task.

After quiet was restored, a warrior stepped out from the lines saying, "Queen, we are very happy to do this; we who have lived in this valley know full well how all suffer from the uncheckable north winds."

The queen escorted the old couple back to their humble cottage and sat with them until her stalwart braves returned with the green-tipped poles. It looked like another Birnam Wood in the process of locomotion. The work

PENN'S CAVE HOTEL

was so quickly and carefully done that it seemed almost like a miracle to the wretched old Indians. They fell on their knees, kissing the hem of their queen's garment and thanking her for her beneficence. She could hardly leave them, so profuse were they in their gratitude. In all but a few hours were consumed in granting what to her was a simple favor, and she was safe and sound within her royal lodge house by dark. Before she left, she had promised to return when the corn crop was ripe and partake of a com roast with the venerable couple. The old people hardly dared hope she would come, but those about her knew that her word was as good as her bond. That night bonfires were lit to celebrate her return, and there was much Indian music and revelry.

Nitanee was compelled to address the frenzied mob, and in her speech, she told them that while they had won a great victory, she hoped it would be the last while she lived; she hated war but would give her life rather than have her people invaded. All she asked in this world was peace with honor. That expressed the sentiment of her people exactly, and they literally went mad with loyalty and enthusiasm for the balance of the night. Naturally, with such an uproar, there was no sleep for Nitanee.

As she lay awake on her couch, she thought that far sweeter than victory or earthly fame was helping others, the smoothing of rough pathways for the weak or oppressed. She resolved more than ever to dedicate her life to benefiting her subjects. No love affair had come into her life; she would use her great love—nature—to put brightness into unhappy souls about her. And she got up the next morning much more refreshed than she could have after a night of sleep surcharged with dreams of victory and glory.

As the summer progressed and the corn crop in the valleys became ripe, the queen sent an orderly to notify the aged couple that she would come to their home alone the next evening for the promised corn roast. It was a wonderful, calm, cloudless night, with the full moon shedding its effulgent smile over the plain. Unaccompanied, except by her orderly, Nitanee walked to the modest cabin of the aged couple, a distance of about five miles, for the cottage stood not far from the present village of Linden Hall. Evidently, the windbreak had been a success, for, bathed in moonlight, the tasseled heads of the cornstalks appeared above the tops of the cedar hedge. Smoke was issuing from the open hearth back of the hut, which showed that the roast was being prepared. The aged couple was delighted to see her, and the evening passed, bringing innocent and supreme happiness to all. And thus, in broad unselfishness and generosity of thought and deed, the great queen's life was spent, making her pathway through her realm radiant with sunshine.

And when she came to die, after a full century of life, she requested that her body be laid to rest in the royal forest, in the center of the valley whose people she loved and served so well. Her funeral cortege, which included every person in the plains and valleys, a vast assemblage, shook with common grief. It would be hard to find a successor like her, a pure soul so deeply animated with true godliness.

And it came to pass that on the night she was buried beneath a modest mound covered with cedar boughs, and the vast funeral party had dispersed, a terrific storm arose, greater than even the oldest person could remember. The blackness of the night was intense; the roar and rumbling heard made every being fear that the end of the world had come. It was a night of intense terror, of horror. But at dawn, the tempest abated, only a gentle breeze remained, golden sunlight overspread the scene, and great was the wonder thereof. In the center of the vast plain where Nitanee had been laid away stood a moundlike mountain, a towering, sylvan giant covered with dense groves of cedar and pine. And as it stood there, eternal, it tempered and broke the breezes from the north, promising new prosperity, greater tranquility, to the peaceful dwellers in the vale that has since been called John Penn's Valley, after the grandson of William Penn.

A miracle, a sign of approval from the Great Spirit, had happened during the night to keep forever alive the memory of Nitanee, who had tempered the winds from the corn patch of the aged, helpless couple of years before. And the dwellers in the valleys adjacent to Mount Nittany awoke to a greater pride in themselves; a high ideal must be observed since they were the special objects of celestial notice.

And the name of Nitanee was the favorite cognomen for Indian maidens and has been borne by many of saintly and useful life ever since, and none of these namesakes were more deserving than the Nitanee who lived centuries later near the mouth of Penn's Cave.

XI

A VISIT TO HOWE'S CAVE,
NEW YORK, 1919

NOW is the time to visit caves! Take this straight from one who knows. Do not delay, as you may be too late. Already the quarries have made a sorry mess of the weird world-famed Howe's Cave in Schoharie County, New York. It was with high hopes that the writer planned a trip to Howe's Cave this summer. He had wanted to visit ever since, years ago, he saw an old lithograph showing Horace Greeley's visit to the cave during his presidential campaign in 1872; the great editor, in his familiar wide-awake hat and linen duster, was surrounded by a group of black-bearded dignitaries, rendered still more impressive by flat-brimmed beaver hats and flowing Prince Albert coats. Several ladies, with the cherry-box hats and cashmere shawls of the period, stood peering into the yawning chasm's mouth. From the caption below, Greeley was evidently of the opinion that Howe's Cave was the world's eighth wonder. *Sic transit gloria mundi!*

Today all is changed. Properly speaking, there is no Howe's Cave, though the name still lives on in the railway station and the post office. The Hederberg Cement

Company set off a blast that caused the vaulted, stalactite roof to fall in, creating chaos and forever shutting out the public from the mysterious depths and labyrinths of this famous cavern. At least so we were told by an employee of the Cement Company, who, in a reminiscent mood, recounted the stories of the cave's former popularity before the Cement Company took charge and blasted away what took God a million years to make in five fell seconds!

The handsome limestone hotel, with its high Mansard roof, which in its day harbored noted men and women from all over the world—Henry Ward Beecher and Harriet Beecher Stowe, General Grant, Horatio Seymour, Jenny Lind, the Prince of Wales, afterward King Edward VII; Dr. Kane, the Arctic explorer; Ida Isaacs Menken, the dancer; Belle Boyd, Roscoe Conkling, Governor Sprague and his wife, Kate Chase Sprague, Governor Stanford, of California, and, of course, Greeley—persons whom we have heard our grandparents talk of familiarly, still stands, but now the office of the Cement Trust.

The click of the typewriters comes through the open windows, where the voices of eager and enthusiastic tourists once reverberated. The elecampane weed grows rank about the walks and gardens; the iron fences are awry. Howe's Cave is no more; it has joined the long procession of defunct natural wonders.

The Palisades, along the Hudson River in New York, came near going the same way; so did the giant trees in California, and here in Pennsylvania, we all know what the stone men have done to Jack's Narrow's on the Juniata River, and to Mount Penn, in the environs of Reading.

John D. Mishler, Reading's first citizen, loves to tell how, when he showed a delegation of distinguished Japanese the wonders of the Berks County metropolis, Baron Ito remarked: "How marvelous are you Americans! I perceive that you are blasting away that vast mountain because, doubtless, it obscures your view to the east."

Someone in a sotto voice whispered: "No; it's only local quarrymen getting out ballast and building stone."

And all this shows that caves and all natural wonders should be taken over by the government, just as during the world war, it took railroads, steamboats, and wheat, and with the natural wonders would ensure the permanency of sights that are a joy and an education to generations unborn.

But as this millennium has not arrived, and is a long way off, take straight advice and see your caves now, as most of them are in limestone countries and already viewed with jealous eyes by corporate interests.